Alaska Unsalted

Tales of Life and Death on the Last Frontier

Bill Miles

Bear Creek Press

Praise for Bill Miles' ALASKA UNSALTED

"Take a wild ride through an unexpected Alaska of funeral parlors, bingo halls, and gay charity balls. Bill Miles' stories startle with their originality while reminding us of what it means—and takes—to be human." – Nancy Lord, author of *The Man Who Swam with Beavers, Green Alaska,* and *Beluga Days*

"Bill Miles is the true voice of the Northwest, a writer who walks with Bret Harte, Jack London, Nelson Algren, and James T. Farrell. These stories from cold places are shapely, funny, suspenseful, wise, and unforgettable." – Sterling Watson, author *of Blind Tongues, Deadly Sweet,* and *Sweet Dream Baby*

"Bill Miles has a gift for using closely observed detail to illuminate character. And what remarkable characters they are in this collection—people so quirky and individual that Alaska seems their perfect setting, a natural habitat." – Marcia Preston, Editor & Publisher of *ByLine* magazine and author of *Perhaps She'll Die, Song of the Bone*s, and *The Butterfly House*

"In *Alaska Unsalted*, Bill Miles brings the eye of an anthropologist and the ear of a natural storyteller to bear on the grand human comedy that is his subject. Take a spin around the floor with Mrs. Remarque and the other characters in this collection, my friend. You won't regret it." – Jack Miles, Pulitzer Prize-winning author of *God: A Biography*

"These tales, told with straight-faced humor and great affection for the flawed and occasionally doomed people, portray a love of the natural landscape of the area, and a sly understanding of the human heart anywhere." – Peter Meinke, Flannery O'Connor Award-winning author of *The Piano Tuner*

"These stories offer insights into unique Alaskans responding to life and destiny. The well-crafted originality of these individuals frequently provide haunting surprises." – Patricia Roppel, author of *Salmon from Kodiak* and *Fortunes from the Earth*

"Bill Miles sprinkles whimsical styles with substance to flavor his Alaskan vignettes. I savored them all—you will, too." – Jay S. Hammond, former Alaska governor and author of *Chips from the Chopping Block: More Tales from Alaska's Bush Rat Governor*

unsalted *adj.* **1.** Meat not seasoned or cured. **2.** A mine not laced with phony gold. **3.** A winter road lacking an ice-thawing agent. **4.** Stories without pretense.

Alaska Unsalted

Tales of Life and Death on the Last Frontier

Published by
Bear Creek Press
814 Couch Avenue • Wallowa, Oregon 97885
541-886-9020 • bearcreekpress@eoni.com
www.bearcreekpress.com

Printing History

Versions of stories in this collection have appeared in the following publications: "The Strength of His Ancestors," *Creative Reading*, January/February 1993, and *Explorations*, March 1997; "A Rube's Game," *Fine Print*, December 1997; "Sister Skagway," *The Klondike Gold Rush Anthology*, 1997; "A Year of Muktuk," *bananafish*, Fall/Winter 1998; "Gabriel's Gift," *ByLine*, May 2000; "Henry Bozek's Perfect Lawn," *Writer's Journal*, November/December 2001, and *The MacGuffin*, Spring 2002; "Dancing with Mrs. Remarque," *ByLine*, October 2003. In addition, the following stories have won awards in fiction writing contests: "Gabriel's Gift" (*Writer's Digest* Fiction Contest, 1997), "Sister Skagway" (*Byline Magazine's* Short Fiction Contest, 1997), "A Rube's Game" (*Authors-in-the Park* Short Story Contest, 1997), and "Dancing with Mrs. Remarque" (*Writer's Digest* Fiction Writing Contest, 2001; nominated for the Pushcart Prize, 2003).

Bear Creek Press First Edition, May 2004

Front cover
From "Fields of Cover," a watercolor by Rebecca Biddle Wood Hardesty of Boise, Idaho
Phone: 208-389-9318 • E-mail: gitogether@aol.com

Printed in the United States of America.

ISBN: 1-930111-43-6

Bear Creek Press

World Headquarters located in Wallowa, Oregon U.S.A.
(at the old Abbie Riggle place on Bear Creek Road).

To Sterling Watson—
writer, teacher, friend.

ACKNOWLEDGMENTS

My thanks go out to Linda Fink, Julie Krafft, Pat Roppel, and Lee Stoops for insightful criticism;

to Marcia Preston and the staff at *ByLine* for publishing two of the stories, and for nominating "Dancing with Mrs. Remarque" for the Pushcart Prize;

and to Mark Highberger of Bear Creek Press for noble publishing heroics and a spirited sense of humor.

Contents

Dancing with Mrs. Remarque

Agnes Dombrowski Smeltzer, the youngest and homeliest of the seven Dombrowski daughters, despised Mrs. Chester A. Remarque for her over-bearing ways and gaudy make-up. Over the years, Mrs. Remarque had troweled on layers of face powder and rouge in what Agnes saw as a hysterical attempt to remain young. She slathered on her Royal Volcano lipstick, neither coloring within the lines of her lips nor avoiding her teeth.

Her nails, however, were done to perfection at Cut 'n Curl. They blazed like tiny highway flares. Her toes glowed in the same grotesque color. Always Royal Volcano. Every week, Mrs. Remarque repeated the same line, "Any woman can have her fingernails done; true elegance demands matching toes."

During Agnes' first year out of high school, she spent her days giving manicures and pedicures at the Cut 'n Curl and her nights taking courses at the Alaska College of Beautification and Cosmetology. Although she flunked the beautician's licensure exam, she learned to shape hair as well as any of the girls in the shop.

Early in her Cut 'n Curl career, she'd been told to give Mrs. Remarque a pedicure in preparation for the Fur Rendezvous parade. Dutifully, Agnes soaked the old lady's right foot in warm water and massaged it with skin softener. When she brushed cuticle remover onto Mrs. Remarque's big toe, a drop ran onto the toe's knuckle. The old lady stiffened and, not accidentally, kicked Agnes under the chin. "Watch your ways, child," Mrs. Remarque chided.

"Sorry, Mrs. R. Sorry."

"You're not only homely as a jar of paste, you're as oafish as a dwarf."

The comparison to a jar of paste was accurate. Agnes knew her head was shaped more like a shoebox than a smooth oval of the pretty girls. Her skin was gray and freckled, her complexion as lumpy as oatmeal. And then there was the mole.

Agnes shook at the rebuke. She applied the Royal Volcano to Mrs. Remarque's left big toe, too nervous to have remembered the skin softener or the cuticle remover. The old lady screamed for the manager. Helena sent Agnes to the back room to clean hair brushes. At the day's end, Helena comforted Agnes. "The old biddy's toes are more important to her than anything else. It has something to do with her view of breeding and class. Don't worry yourself, child. You'll learn." Agnes always looked on the incident as her Grand Martyrdom.

On Thanksgiving night four years later, Agnes again readied herself for an appointment with Mrs. Remarque, this time at Lombardo's Division Street Funeral Parlor. The old lady was as dead as a clod of dirt.

When Agnes had told Jerry about the funeral-home job opening, he swore he'd leave her. Her six sisters urged her to start the next day—before he changed his mind. Agnes said to Jerry, "It's seven-to-one against you." She didn't care what he thought. He was a disease she'd cure and Lombardo's was the medicine. Within weeks, she had moved back in with her parents.

Her father said, "Divorce is out of the question. Not for my baby. Not for a good Catholic girl."

"Divorce, annulment—who cares? I'd prefer murder. I don't give a moose's tooth one way or another. Jerry and I are *kaput*."

"You still wear his earrings every day."

Agnes caressed the pearls Jerry had given her as a wedding present. "They were the one decent thing he did for me in three years. They're genuine."

"But," her father protested, "they won't help you find another husband. You had to wait nineteen years for this one, such as he is." Then he asked, "Do you have another prospect we don't know of? Remember, child, Jerry is the man for whom you saved yourself."

It had not been difficult to save herself for marriage—Jerry Smeltzer was the only man ever to ask her out and even then showed little interest in robbing her of anything. She was a virgin on her wedding day and felt like a virgin after three years of marriage.

To induce Agnes into the funeral parlor business, Mr. Lombardo had phoned her daily at Cut 'n Curl. Would she be interested in a career with advancement potentialities? Would she like a job with a generous salary? A flexible work schedule? Good training? During Agnes' visit to the funeral home, Mr. Lombardo rapped on the top of a middle-of-the-line bronze casket and said that she would not have to see so much as an unclothed arm. Yet she could take the utmost pride in the knowledge that her hands would be the last to touch many of her fellow parishioners. "It's almost like the eighth sacrament or the eleventh commandment, my dear," he said.

He admitted that she'd sometimes be called to work holidays. Thus far, he joked, neither medical science nor the Good Lord made people die according to any time clock. But she'd have more than ample time to pursue whatever hobbies a plain girl like her enjoyed. And best of all, no customer ever talked back. As a bonus, he'd try a couple of the cosmetic secrets on her that he'd learned in thirty-seven years. Just sand away some of that acne and snip off the mole. She declined the surgery but accepted the job.

At a family dinner to celebrate Agnes' unmarried status, the oldest Dombrowski sister was elected to organize a series of dates for Agnes. Each brother-in-law was required to come up with two single Catholic friends or face the scorn of the entire clan. Agnes swore that she would date no man chosen by the family. Period. Paragraph. End of chapter. Her protestations were unneeded. When candidates learned that Aggie had once been married and was, therefore, not the freshest salmon in the river, most dove for the gravel beds. The two who'd hung on, upon hearing about her job as a mortician's assistant, rode away on the second tide.

Tony Lombardo's Division Street Funeral Parlor was also his home. He and his wife, Dolly, raised three children on the second floor. He had turned the ground-level apartment into two visitation chapels.

In the basement he displayed casket samples and built what he called The Lab. The bereaved never saw The Lab but it was the part of the building in which Mr. Lombardo took the most pride. He had converted a coal shed into a dazzling white ceramic monument to professional embalming, going so far as to install the latest 1950s drainage system—linked directly to the Anchorage sewer system—under each of the twin stainless steel tables.

The walls glistened with floor-to-ceiling white ceramic tile. Two stainless-steel sinks had been built into a wall-to-wall counter. An eye-level boardwalk of shelving held gallons of embalming chemicals, soaps, and lotions. Over each gleaming table hung a fluorescent shop fixture. With both fixtures lighted, the room throbbed in immaculate brightness—except for the floor, re-painted every six months in fresh coal-black enamel.

Mr. Lombardo saw himself as the operator of a finishing school. He called each corpse, male or female, his "date." The date would emerge from finishing school impeccably groomed for a wake, called a "dance." A funeral was a "prom." He personally performed all the routine embalming services and dressed each date. His assistant finished the hair and make-up, and affixed any jewelry the family had chosen. Mr. Lombardo paid the assistant for an extra half-hour if the date was a woman. Nails took time.

In addition, Mr. Lombardo prepared a cigar box for each date. It held any personal effects to be worn by the deceased as well as a white index card with biographical highlights. Agnes tucked Mrs. Remarque's card into a corner of a mirror. "Time to go to work," she said to the mirror. "Freckles are not all that ugly. Freckles are *not* ugly!" She told herself that her scabby mole wasn't ugly but never believed it. The few boys drawn to look at her studied the mole before checking out her figure. Their eyes always returned to the mole.

Standing over Mrs. Remarque, Agnes waved her hands like a magician and snatched the bed sheet away. "To work, to work," she said.

The Baby Ben on the shelf told her it was almost midnight. "How are you this fine Thanksgiving Day, Mrs. Remarque? Do you remember me? I tried to give you a pedicure back at Cut 'n Curl. You gave me the devil in front of Helena and all the girls. You called me 'homely' and 'oafish.' I cried my way home that night."

In the raspy voice Agnes used for a cadaver's reply, Mrs. Remarque said, "Why, no, dear Agnes, I don't remember that at all. I'm so sorry. You're a lovely child." Agnes smiled.

Mrs. Remarque said, "Do you think we could have music?"

Agnes switched on the radio and drummed her fingers on the steel sink as the tubes warmed up. She joined the song in progress:

How much is that doggie in the window,
The one with the waggledy tail?
How much is that doggie in the window?
I do hope that doggie's for sale.

Mr. Lombardo had warned Agnes about Mrs. Remarque's dress. It was a milky-white silk number with oversized vermilion roses, showy yet elegant. To touch it was like touching cream. Mrs. Remarque's lawyer had sent it by cab. Mr. Lombardo said it came with matching lipstick and nail polish. Agnes remembered the Royal Volcano.

She wondered what type of person would go so far as to dictate specific burial clothes to a lawyer. Wait till she told her father. Then again, maybe she shouldn't tell him. Why give him another reason to carp about her job? During one of their regular arguments, her father had said that working as a mortician was a sin for a woman, a Mortal Sin. Her immortal soul would be damned to the fires of hell forever. For proof, he called Monsignor Parker. The Monsignor said he would look into the question, but he never called back.

Agnes folded Mrs. Remarque's arms across her stomach. "You're warmer than my usual dates, Mrs. R. Has Mr. Lombardo been smooching on you, or did he just leave you out of the fridge too long? You mustn't become faint." Agnes checked the wall thermometer. "Fifty-two degrees. A perfect temperature for you, Mrs. R."

"Yes," the raspy voice agreed. "Splendid weather we're having."

"Splendid? That's a splendid word, Mrs. R."

The disc jockey introduced *Two To Tango*. Agnes took Mrs. Remarque's hand. "May I have this dance?"

"Of course," came the raspy reply. Agnes started a jitterbug holding tightly to Mrs. Remarque's limp hand.

"We have to do something about these nails," Agnes said. "You were always so particular." Agnes ducked under Mrs. Remarque's arm and twirled. The dance step pulled Mrs. Remarque's dress up her thighs. Her nylon stockings were rolled like sausages just below the knees. Agnes dropped the hand. "My, my, Mrs. R," she said, rearranging the dress, "modesty at all times. What would the cronies in the Altar and Rosary Society say if they saw such behavior?"

"I can't help myself," Mrs. Remarque rasped.

"How well I know." Agnes tucked a white barber's towel under Mrs. Remarque's chin. "Time for your facial."

She squeezed a line of beige paste into her palm and worked it into Mrs. Remarque's face, turning her slightly tan. She patted pink powder over the paste and worked it into all the creases until the old lady's skin took on a smooth sheen. Agnes repeated the procedure for each of Mrs. Remarque's hands. Then she polished the old lady's cheeks from a pink rouge cake. "I'll have you gorgeous in no time flat, Mrs. R. A real train-stopper. But no toes. Not from this Cinderella. You're going to meet your maker with bare-naked, unpolished feet."

"Such a shame," Mrs. Remarque said.

Agnes rifled through the cigar box: diamond bracelet, Lady Elgin watch, silver locket, eyeglasses, felt-backed Sacred Heart scapular—jewelry for eternity. "But no earrings," she said. "Strange."

Agnes read Mrs. Remarque's biography from the index card. "Born in 1892; died in 1953. That makes you…over sixty. And isn't this interesting? You have two sons: Charlie, the director of a school for the deaf, and John, who died in World War I. God must have known you were going to snitch on me for messing up your pedicure, or else He would have spared him. It's amazing He gave you kids at all." The card also said that Mrs. Remarque was a third-order Franciscan. "Maybe you aren't such a monster." She flipped the card into the cigar box. "Interesting, but now it's time for your finishing touches."

She fluffed Mrs. Remarque's hair, like tossing salad with her hands. "This won't take long." She snapped into place two rollers, short, pink logs buried in white sand. With a can of hair spray, she cemented Mrs. Remarque's hair into place and then shot two quick bursts at the old lady's feet. "So much for your oafish toes."

The first trick-of-the-trade that she had learned from Mr. Lombardo was the application of lip color. With a razor blade, Mr. Lombardo showed her how to shave onionskin-thin tissues of lipstick into a small stone mortar. She dripped an equal amount of wax from a lighted candle into the mortar and finished the recipe by adding no more than five drops of three-in-one oil. She ground the ingredients into a paste. "If you mix it too watery," Mr. Lombardo had said, "and the chapel gets warm, the color runs like spit. Too thick, it cracks and crumbles, leaving your date's lips looking like they've been coated with Rice Krispies."

Later, as she worked with Mr. Lombardo on a real person, he had said, "Another secret—lights never shine directly on a date. Even though she may be the belle of the ball, so to speak, no spotlight. In our lab, we can make her look better than she looked in life. We can also make her look much better than plain dead. What we can't do is make her look alive. I know you saw that new 3-D movie, *House of Wax*. The statues don't look alive, do they?" Agnes had to agree.

Now, Agnes slipped a wooden tongue depressor between Mrs. Remarque's lips. "Say aaaaagh." She tugged at a corner of the old lady's mouth, tightening the lips. Then she brushed on the mixture, first the upper lip and then the lower. The mixture congealed. Mr. Lombardo told her to move the lips quickly until the date took on a prayerful look that said, *I am at peace*. Neither joyful nor sorrowful. Just asleep. A second coating would enhance the color and solidify the shape of the lips, rendering them immobile, the jaw operational only with the use of crow bar.

Agnes painted on the second coat. With her pinkie, she touched the left corner of the mouth and curled it downward. "You don't want to look like you're laughing, Mrs. R. In life, you never did that."

The radio began playing *The Hokey Pokey*. "Another dance, Mrs. R?" She lifted the old lady's hand and sang:

You put your left hand in,
You put your left hand out,
You put your left hand in
And you shake it all about…

The song ended and Agnes recalled Mr. Lombardo's comment about *House of Wax*. At the sink counter, she rummaged through her purse, surfacing with her cardboard 3-D glasses. It had been months since she'd seen the movie, but the glasses still went everywhere with her. She dropped to her hands and knees and crawled back to Mrs. Remarque, kneeling upright to peek over the woman's shoulder. "Boo!"

She noticed that Mrs. Remarque's ears had been pierced. "So are mine," she said, touching her pearls. "It's so strange the lawyer didn't send earrings over. Isn't that just like a man."

She slipped the 3-D glasses onto Mrs. Remarque. "Don't we look peachy now."

The green cellophane lenses and pink rollers turned Mrs. Remarque into a Ringling clown. If the old lady had ever wanted a disguise, this was it. Glasses, rollers and wax lips. The pope could be under all that and no one would recognize him.

Agnes shook the bottle of Royal Volcano as the radio played *Stranger In Paradise*. "Oh, you're any place but paradise, Mrs. R. Can you hear me?" she shouted at a pierced ear. "You're in Mr. Lombardo's basement. On a steel slab! Dead as a brick!"

For no reason she could think of, Agnes sat down on the black concrete floor and began sobbing. The sobs turned to tears and the tears flowed down her cheeks, dropping off her chin and running into the drain. Without thinking, she reached up for the hem of Mrs. Remarque's dress and dabbed at her eyes. "Stop," she said. "Stop it this instant, you boob."

Agnes dried her face on her sweatshirt sleeve and reached under the table for an Easter basket: tweezers, eyebrow pencils, and lash curlers; cuticle scissors, nail buffers, and manicure sticks; a variety of nippers and clippers. She balanced the basket in the center of Mrs. Remarque's stomach and selected a metal nail file.

Since those first days at Cut 'n Curl, Agnes had attended to her own fingernails with saintly zeal. She may have been born trash-sack homely with an eye-popping mole and ears capable of lifting her off the ground like the Virgin Mary's own Ascension, but her fingers drew raves. Not a millimeter of dead cuticle anywhere. The nails were all exactly one-quarter inch long, buffed and polished and shaped at least three times a week. On Saturday nights, with nothing better to do, Agnes lounged in her bathtub, removed the weekly treatments and massaged her hands with Colgate Tooth Powder. Her hands felt purified.

Agnes lifted Mrs. Remarque's hand and held the old lady's thumb next to her own. The women were a thousand years apart in age but there was no difference in their thumbs. The nails were clipped to the same quarter inch, shaped to perfection and free of ridges. They had been coated with polish and covered in a clear, protective gloss. Agnes pressed Mrs. Remarque's thumb to her lips: cold.

"Enough," Agnes said. "Never mind that you were a witch in life. Never mind that your nails are almost as fine as mine. I shall make them…perfect. Queenly."

An hour later, Agnes checked the wall clock. "Two a.m.! My God, Mr. Lombardo will pitch a fit." Agnes blew on Mrs. Remarque's right-hand pinkie to set the top coat of clear polish. Then she snapped on the hair dryer "We just won't tell him I spent all this time on you. Our secret, okay, Mrs. R?"

"Okay," the raspy voice said. "You do splendid work, my dear."

"Think so?" Agnes said. "By golly, you're right. Thank you."

"You're welcome," Mrs. Remarque said.

Agnes said, "Let's see: hair...check. Make up...check. Nails...check and double check. You should be proud of those hands, Mrs. R. You should be modeling for Cartier instead of going to your prom."

"The toes," Agnes rasped in Mrs. Remarque's voice.

"No one will see your toes," Agnes said.

"Do my toes."

"Mr. Lombardo would kill me for wasting time on something no one is going to see."

"The toes. Elegance demands matching toes."

"No!" Turning her back on Mrs. Remarque, Agnes sifted through the cigar box again, withdrawing the silver locket. Inside, a miniature brown-toned daguerreotype of a young woman no more than eighteen looked back at her. Perhaps a daughter's high-school graduation picture? A wedding picture? The young woman had tight, short hair and a nose disfigured with a knurl the color and shape of a kidney bean. A prominent scar ran below her lower lip as if she had completely bitten though the flesh.

Agnes studied the picture, then Mrs. Remarque's face: the faint trail of a scar. The picture was of Mrs. Remarque. With a mole on her nose! Agnes slipped the locket around her own neck.

"The toes," Mrs. Remarque said. Agnes hadn't touched them since the Grand Martyrdom. It made no sense to do them now. She was late as it was. Mr. Lombardo would never pay so much overtime.

But then, Mrs. Remarque was going to her prom; it was her last dance. "Damn," Agnes said.

Agnes aimed the hair dryer at Mrs. Remarque's toes until they became warm and pliable. She peeled down the old lady's stockings, washed her feet and massaged them with skin softener. Then the cuticle remover and two coats of Royal Volcano. "Our secret, Mrs. R. Mr. Lombardo will never know."

"Thank you, child."

"You are awash in beauty, Mrs. R, but somehow…incomplete."

Agnes unclasped her pearl earrings and touched each to her lips. She fitted a post through Mrs. Remarque's cold earlobe, her fingers twittering like hummingbird wings. "Steady, damn it!"

The pearls transformed Mrs. Remarque into royalty. "May I have this dance?" Agnes asked, and kissed Mrs. Remarque lightly on the cheek.

She signed out at 1 a.m., donned the 3-D glasses, and ascended the basement stairs to Division Street.

A Year of Muktuk

Nola Tutuliak balanced herself atop the build-up of ridge ice, one foot on each side of its crest. Gnarled ice crags rose three stories high and ran as far along the shore as her vision carried. She visored her eyes with her hands and focused on the whale. A hundred yards away, its tail was tethered to the thin shelf ice that separated land from water; its head pointed seaward as if it were ready to swim back into the black depths of the Chukchi.

The sea always fought man to protect her bowhead. The elders spoke of times when the whales were plentiful and villagers harvested them freely. Now, the government did the protecting, allowing Nola's people only one per year. And still, the sea fought ferociously to keep each one, often taking men's lives in revenge.

Nola faced the village, a half-mile inland over the crushed and broken ice mountains. Behind its four neat rows of tottering shacks, summer's salmon still hung in strips on glazed clotheslines, flat bronze icicles waiting to be made into food for the dogs. Warm air and smoke from tin chimneys rose and dissolved into the sub-zero Arctic air. Inside the shacks, boots stood clustered around pot-bellied stoves. Clothes lay draped over ropes angled across the rooms; the dampness kept the windows covered in frost. Nola's second born slept as Grammy T watched. So warm inside, she thought. Tommy had arrived home safely. Tonight they would share themselves.

The tops of Nola's ears burned when she thought intimate thoughts about her husband. She allowed a secret smile, almost able to feel Tommy's calloused hand making its circle around her face. "My pretty pumpkin," he'd said a thousand times. She blushed every time, recognizing the odd roundness to her face, knowing that his hands would begin to cover the rest of her body. Now, her ears revealed her thoughts. She pulled the parka hood over her head.

Soon Tommy would raise the victory flag over their house. A successful hunt. The village would have food and oil for another year.

Tommy's Reeboks gripped the bowhead's black hump like golf shoes. No feeling remained in his left foot; both calves were knotted in cramps. He'd been standing for three sleepless days and nights, at first waiting silently in the bow of the skin boat for the whale to surface. He'd driven the eight-foot harpoon deeply into the whale's back, the barb's explosive charge sending up a puff of red mist. A second and third harpoon landed. Within hours, the creature lost all strength. Tommy led his crew back to the village, dodging ice mountains more massive than the fifty-ton whale in tow.

His brown eyes were slits. His right hand barely had the strength to hold the bull horn. His left rubbed an ivory horseshoe, the good luck charm Nola had pinned to the halo of his California Angels' baseball cap before he'd left. A swirl of spring snowdust funneled in front of his face. He'd struck and killed the whale but hadn't landed her yet. And this year his father wasn't around. The village depended on him alone. If he didn't get her on shore before the tide went out, she'd have to stay in the water for another day and the flesh would spoil, turn sour and not even be fit for the dogs.

He shivered and pulled on a pair of brown cotton work gloves. Looking seaward, he saw a fog bank rolling toward land like an invasion force. In an hour, he'd lose the sun. The tide would ebb four feet below the thin shelf ice. Then the villagers would never be able to drag the bowhead from the water. He had to move now.

Tommy scanned the shore for Nola. A glimpse would be enough. After being away, seeing her the first time would make his throat thick. He'd be proud to have her see him standing triumphantly on the huge hump, a successful captain on the bridge of a long, gray-black submarine. During the slow return trip to the village, Tommy had used visions of Nola to keep himself awake. Now, he squinted along the line of shore ice, but his eyes did not find her among the old women and toddlers who rode the ridge's crest.

With binoculars he searched beyond the ridge to the village. He saw the men honing their knives in preparation for the long night of bloody work. He wished they were able to hitch their pickups and snowmobiles to the whale's tether, but the rough pack ice kept the machines too far from the sea. Parka-clad women scurried about, readying fifty-five gallon drums in which to cook the bowhead's layers of fat into a rich, oily mush. Teenagers harnessed dogs to the sleds to haul the chunks of *muktuk* to each of the houses. But he could not find his wife.

A boy of seven or eight ran to the whale and jabbed a knife in her tail fluke. Tommy hollered the boy away, then carefully slid down the arc of her spine to her tail, smoothed the gash with his bare hand, and clambered back to the top of the hump.

The fluke was partially frozen, a bad sign. Even one night's delay in butchering meant the meat would sour, that his people—his sons and wife—would go without their winter's supply of rich *muktuk*. If he lost the bowhead in the ebbing tide and she drifted back to sea, he'd be shamed. They'd have no oil for cooking or for their lamps, no baleen for scrimshaw.

Tommy raised the bull horn. "CREWS READY?" Two parallel haul lines ran from the flukes across the hundred yards of shelf ice. They disappeared over the ridge of shore ice. The ropes went taut as eight dozen men and women prepared to drag the animal from the water.

An hour before, fifty villagers pulling on a single line had failed to get her onto the shelf ice. Tommy had ordered two lines hooked up to block-and-tackle rigs. He had also ordered ashore the men in the skin boats and skiffs. He needed their strength on land. He sent the young boys, his older son included, to the boats.

Tommy saw Nola running along the shelf ice toward the whale. He lowered the bull horn and the lines went slack.

Nola cupped her tiny hands. "Where's the beer, Captain? We can't have the party without the beer!"

"At Albert's," he hollered back. Then added, "And don't call me 'Captain.'" He was proud to have captained the crew—his first—and prouder still to have brought home the big bowhead. But to be called Captain reddened his face, made him feel like she was trying to brag about the kill. He shouted to her, "What are you staring at?"

"You," she said. "Our hero—Captain." She giggled.

"Get back there and grab a rope!" He waved her to a position at the front of one of the lines. Tommy studied the level of the Chukchi. It was already a foot below the shelf ice.

"Damn!" If the tide fell much more, a thousand villagers wouldn't be able to get the bowhead on shore.

He pressed his fists into the sockets of his eyes—anything to clear his head. He wanted to party with Nola. To raise the victory flag over his house. To get drunk easily, quickly, and fall asleep. He visualized the elders nodding their approval, the toddlers sneaking up to touch the wolf hem of his white Gore-Tex. But only if he finished the job.

He raised the bull horn again. "READY?" The lines tightened, the two block-and-tackles moaned against the solid oak spools on their pulley rings.

"HOLD IT. HOLD IT." He pointed toward the right side of the enormous black tail. "SIX OF YOU—SWITCH SIDES." A dozen bodies scrambled under the line; five moved back as quickly. "THAT'S GOOD." The lines tightened again and the whale's tail rose from the ice. "ON MY SIGNAL."

Like a musical conductor, he pointed at the lines of bodies over which he towered. Then he pointed to the bobbing boats attached to the jaw. He slashed his free hand downward. Four old men sitting on the ice began to pound skin drums with their bare hands. The drummers set a cadence that, later, they would dance to, chanting the old chants. A chorus of muffled grunts echoed in the still air. The tail lifted clear of the ice.

"PULL! PULL!" Tommy felt the whale quiver under his feet, but it did not move toward the shore. "MORE PEOPLE. MORE PEOPLE." Women and old men from the crest of the ice berm scrambled down the incline.

Goddammit, Tommy thought. Last year, the village had taken its whale, a little *inutuq*. He'd been one of the crew, had thrown the second harpoon. His father, then the captain, had managed to get her out of the water on the first try. But she was only twenty-eight tons. And the village had run out of meat and oil months ago. This one would last them all year—unless he failed.

Nola ran toward him a second time. "Are the lines strong enough to bear all these pairs of hands?"

"Back to your place!" He dismissed her with another wave. He hated to treat her like that but the entire village was watching. She scurried back to the front of a line.

The skiffs and skin boats were gathered around the enormous muzzle of the bowhead. Had the whale been alive, she'd be able to bite any boat in half—or crush anyone with a swish of her flukes.

He raised his arm again. "READY?"

The lines stretched. The tail lifted. Tommy dropped his arm, and the chorus of grunts sounded again.

"PULL! PULL! PULL!" The right side of the tail stretched like it had been drawn taut over a skinning rack. Tommy feared that the villagers would pull it off the torso.

"STOP! CHECK THE RIGHT PULLEY." He'd have done it himself, but the tide had dropped another foot. Time was gone.

He motioned toward the skin boats, then to the twin lines of villagers on the shelf ice. Nola blew him a kiss. He flicked open his hand, caught the kiss, and sealed it to his cheek. Then he checked to see if anyone had seen him. He raised his hand again. "READY!" The haul lines tightened. The tail rose. "NOW!" The bowhead's tail stretched and she began to move…slowly…by…inches…up onto the ice. "PULL. PULL. PULL." The drummers speeded the cadence to match the urgency in Tommy's voice.

In the water, the boys in the skin boats prodded the whale's jaw with their oars. The skiff skippers nosed their boats against the whale's muzzle. A boy of fifteen lost his balance and fell into the water. Tommy looked. "PULL!" The boy disappeared. Tommy couldn't stop now. Others needed to care for the boy. The whale was finally moving. This was his job. The boy surfaced, his face white with fear. "PULL!" The boy disappeared again. A wooden oar splashed at the spot where the boy had gone under. When he surfaced, he grabbed the oar; a skin boat glided toward him.

With the bowhead's tail and trunk on the shelf ice, her jaw and flippers angled sharply down into the water. The pulleys groaned, the whale torn between the villagers' need and the determination of the sea.

"PULL!" Tommy yelled. The drummers doubled the beat.

The whale's flippers cleared the water. Soon, her jaw surfaced. The old women and children along the pressure ridge applauded and stomped their feet. Tommy felt a thunk as the jaw crashed onto the ice. He waved the bull horn in a circle over his head. “KEEP GOING! DON’T STOP!” The bowhead was pulled across the shelf ice toward the shore’s pressure ridge. Tommy bellowed encouragement at the villagers as if they were sled dogs working through deep snow. Only fifty yards to solid land.

The first of the haulers climbed the pressure ridge and disappeared over the berm. Tommy saw Nola slip and scramble to her feet without letting loose of the haul line. Her strength had given him two fine sons. She’d delivered them in the village without a doctor or nurse—without a whimper. Their love would bring more children. Now, half the haulers had crossed the ridge. He saw them relaxing, hopping up and down. Too soon.

The bowhead stopped when she reached the base of the ridge. Toddlers bounded down the seaward side of the ridge, peeled off their mittens, and tentatively caressed the sandpaper hide.

Tommy shouted into the bull horn: “ON SHORE! ON SHORE! GET BACK TO THE ROPES!”

From the top of the berm, Nola grinned. Tommy saw her white teeth gleaming. He looked past her, over the berm, to the village. He’d need the dog teams to get the bowhead over the ridge.

“STOP! LOOK UP HERE!” He placed the bull horn on the whale’s back and cracked an imaginary whip. Men ran to their waiting dog teams and unhitched the sleds. Once the dogs had been harnessed to the haul lines, Tommy circled his arm in the air. The sled dogs strained; the bowhead’s tail curved up the grade, then stopped.

“EVERYBODY DOWN ON THE ICE!” The old women and children scrambled down the pack ice and pressed their shoulders against the massive jaw. The ice creaked under the weight as the whale’s body started up the hill.

A line from the right block-and-tackle snapped. The oak spool, as big around as a cannon ball, hurtled back toward the haulers. When it buried itself in Nola’s stomach, her legs and arms folded around it, and she was lifted from her feet and thrown back into the line of haulers. Her lungs collapsed in a muffled gasp. The sharp snap of her spine cracked the Arctic stillness as the haulers stumbled backward. Nola curled into a fetal ball.

Tommy leaped from the whale to the berm's crest and fought his way across the jagged ice to his wife. He pried her hands from the oak spool and eased her body away from the haul line. Her mouth hung open in childlike surprise. He eased it closed and wiped a line of red from her chin. What was he supposed to do now? What *could* he do? He saw his father's image in the ice, then his boys'. Then, he gently placed her head on his Gore-Tex.

The villagers formed a circle, their breath causing a vapor halo around Nola and Tommy. Nola's blood reddened the ice and the villagers backed away, opening the circle as her blood drained toward the sea.

Tommy scooped her lifeless body into his arms and started toward the village. At the base of the berm he placed her on the flat ice, this time covering her with his coat. He pressed his face to the Gore-Tex, seeing nothing but blackness.

Tommy led the villagers back to the whale. He took Nola's place at the head of the towline. "PULL! PULL!" The bowhead climbed the berm, tail first. When her tail cleared the crest, her flukes flapped like black bed sheets drying in a blustery wind. The dogs lunged in their harnesses, and the humped torso of the animal appeared at the top of the ridge.

Finally, her flippers appeared. Then her head. The villagers cheered when she started her downward slide toward them. A half dozen men sprinted toward the village for their knives.

Tommy removed his cap and caressed the horseshoe Nola had given him. The whale was in. He would have an eternity to grieve.

A Rube's Game

"Bingo, by damn!" Little Joe Soto watched Whiskey McCracken throw his left hand into the air to catch the caller's attention. With his right, Whiskey pointed a bingo card at the sign reading TABLE 49. Whiskey always sat at Table 49. Alaska was the 49th state. Lucky 7 times Lucky 7 was 49. Someday, Whiskey said time after time, he'd win enough scratch to get himself a first-class ticket out of Alaska and onto a jet plane headed for Chicago. He'd die in peace and be laid out with his kin.

Joe felt that Whiskey had a brain the size of a thimble and a bladder to match, but he knew the old geezer was no one to mess with in a bingo hall. At eighty, Whiskey was friskier than a pair of foxy forties. He chain-smoked Camels and drank Gatorade, spilling down his shirt as much as he got into his mouth. His dingy-gray cardigan, permanently misbuttoned, smelled like a saloon mop. But in front of Whiskey McCracken stood five tall trophies lined up like a row of saints, testament to the fact that he was best bingo player not only in St. Viator's church basement, but in all of Alaska.

Joe swept the dots from his cards onto the table. No sense waiting for the caller to confirm the win. If Whiskey called bingo, it was in the bank.

The floorwalker near Whiskey's table, an aging Altar and Rosary Society cowgirl whose waist overflowed her three-inch belt, took the old guy's card. She shouted out the card's four-digit serial number. Immediately, the card appeared on the hall's twenty television monitors.

Jimmy Corner, the bingo caller, leaned into the microphone. "That's another win for Whiskey McCracken. Merry Christmas, again, from St. Viator, Whiskey." Jimmy had been calling the games for years and knew all the regulars by name. A thousand people moaned. The church sounded like it would slide off its foundation in pain.

Whiskey tugged at the leather fringe on the attendant's denim shirt, a fringe dangling dangerously close to her heavy bosom. He winked. "You get my money, honey, and shake a leg. This ain't no game for rubes. Then take all these cards back to the card box and fish me out some new luck." He pushed his skinny frame away from the bingo table and stood. Then he thrust his crotch at her. "I'm gonna go drain King Kong. Hah!"

She laughed and blushed. Little Joe could see she was tickled that Whiskey McCracken would trust her to fetch his bingo cards. Other players religiously chose their own cards from the mesh playpens at the main door. Not Whiskey. He broke all the rules. He lit a Camel and sauntered off, pulling his bright red oxygen canister.

Everything about Whiskey riled Joe. The old guy never entered a bingo hall without that damned oxygen tank. In a smoky hall, he said the fresh air kept his thinking sharp and his reflexes fast. Said it was doctor's orders, too, but that they were all quacks, so who knew what was copasetic.

Whiskey was three times older than Joe but always had the women—even the young ones—laughing. Joe's last date had been with a dental assistant from a Seattle escort service. Whiskey, stooped as he was, was still a head taller than Joe. But then, Joe was only four-eleven in elevator shoes; sixth graders were taller. Joe's mother had told him that he was born two months early. That was supposed to explain why he had legs shaped like stubby milk bottles. No, Joe wasn't much to look at, and Whiskey had the women and as well as the luck—but nothing lasted forever.

Every Friday, St. Viator's hosted fifteen-dollar bingo. Half the mopes showed up with a good-luck charm: a picture of the family Husky, a St. Jude scapular, or an ashtray embossed with a shamrock. The other half brought potato chip bags the size of pillowcases, and margarine containers of homemade dip.

On the first Friday of each month, the church raised the buy-in to thirty dollars. Grannies with freshly-permed blue hair and two-hour manicures packed the hall. The last game was always a blackout. To win the thousand-dollar prize, a player needed to cover all twenty-five squares on a card. If successful in forty-five numbers or less, the prize jumped to five thousand dollars. The First Friday Five—the Big F—was Alaska's richest and most popular bingo game. Over four years, the church had paid out the big prize on eight occasions. Whiskey had won it five times. Next year, things would change for Joe Soto, Whiskey McCracken or no Whiskey McCracken.

Before the Big F, Joe always visited the church upstairs and lit candles. He wasn't sure what kind of luck the candles might bring but he'd seen other serious bingo players lighting them. It couldn't hurt. Maybe he'd score some points with God. So far, he was well aware that he'd missed all of Alaska's opportunities to get rich. He hadn't been born during the gold stampede or in whaling days. He'd arrived in Alaska after oil was struck in the '60s and after the pipeline was built in the '70s. He'd even missed the big oil spill when Exxon paid $17.50 an hour—for seven, twelve-hour days—to anyone who could get to Valdez and who was willing to scrub rocks. Joe's luck, he decided, was due to change.

Before Corner began the next game, Monsignor Parker took the stage. He announced a bonus evening of bingo for the Fourth of July. The event would be held at the Egan Center with its capacity of five thousand souls.

Twenty games would be played, *each* with a prize of...one thousand dollars. The faithful oohed and aahed. The big game, a blackout, would be the last of the evening and would carry a grand prize of...ten thousand dollars. If won in forty-five numbers or less, the lucky winner would go home with forty-five thousand dollars.

"That's right," the Monsignor repeated, "forty-five thousand dollars for forty-five in the year of Our Lord 2004." Everyone in the church basement rose and applauded. This, Joe thought, would be *his* game—Whiskey McCracken be damned!

Joe ran up the stairs to the church and lit seven candles. Almost a year back, when he still hadn't won the Big F, he'd stopped stealing the change from the poor box. That alone, he knew, had to be racking up points in his favor. And he was one guy who knew about points. You never bet the odds; you bet points. You gave points; you took points. If you bet the odds, you lost. At the race track, a rube got odds. How many saps lost paychecks every day at tracks all over the world? The gangsters had race tracks wrapped up tighter than St. Ann's legs. Always bet points, Joe figured. That way a guy would win sooner or later.

Kneeling before the bank of votive candles in front of St. Viator's statue, Little Joe started planning for the big game. He'd take his time and line up a team of guys. He'd spend every dime he had for their buy-ins. In swap, he'd take half their winnings and split the rest among everyone even-up. When the big win came, he'd wave the whole wad right in Whiskey McCracken's face. Before anyone was the wiser, he'd be on a red-eye, bound for the tiki bars of Tampa. On a barstool, he was as tall as the next guy.

Back in the church basement, Joe ambled toward the stage. He stood on a milk crate to see inside the plastic hopper holding the bingo balls. He wasn't sure what he was checking, but he liked to see the balls bouncing around. "What's up," he said to Corner.

Corner had a face pitted with acne craters. It reminded Joe of the surface of the moon. But he was a good, religious guy and passed Joe a holy card from time to time. He'd given one to Whiskey earlier. Nothing got by Joe Soto.

Whiskey finally returned from the bathroom, parked his oxygen canister under the table, and adjusted the tubes in his nostrils. He snapped open his Zippo, touched the flame to a cigarette, and waved at Joe, who nodded back. The old bastard was just too damn lucky! Joe knew exactly what he'd do if he ever got his hands on the oxygen tank—and exactly where he'd shove it.

Corner leaned into the microphone and announced the next game, "Four corners, one winner." Joe wandered back toward his seat, his short legs bobbing his body from side to side like a wobbly watermelon rolling down the street.

In March, Whiskey had missed bingo three weeks running. If the old guy was pulling out of the bingo racket, Joe wanted to know why, especially with the big game coming up. It paid to know what was what, especially because Joe already had a dozen guys set for the scam. He didn't want anything to go south. It was worth a visit to Whiskey's place.

Joe found him in his furnished room at the Anchorage Econotel. The room had a two-burner hot plate, a refrigerator as large as a chest of drawers, and its own window. Whiskey was sitting in a bean bag chair under a floor lamp. He was naked from the waist up, holding under his chin an aluminum sun reflector that looked like a pizza pan.

"Cush digs," Joe said, trying to sound friendly. "All the comforts of home."

Whiskey snorted. "I only got to share the toilet with one other guy, so it'll do till something really good comes along. If nothing surfaces, I'll die right here in this bean chair. What'd you come by for?"

"To see why you ain't been to the game."

Whiskey folded the sun disk and pulled on a tank-top undershirt that reached to his navel. "I've had it with them crumb-bum Catholics, and I want the whole world to know. Three years I'm on their pad. I ask for one lousy week off to go to the track in Seattle. They tell me not in the summer, too many tourists show up at the game. I tell them summer is the only time the ponies run at Longacres. I'm their bread and butter guy and they turn me down cold, treat me like a rented mule. Screw them."

"Hold on, hold on. You *work* for St. Viator's and you'd dump 'em for that?"

"That...and the fact that Notre Dame's basketball team didn't come close to covering the spread in their last three games. Screw the Catholics."

"I don't get it."

Whiskey motioned Joe to the porcelain-topped kitchen table. He fitted the oxygen tubes into his nostrils. "You don't think I *play* bingo, do you? I'm a shill. I mean, I *was* a shill. I quit the bastards cold. But don't worry. I wouldn't miss a shot at forty-five G's for my mother's funeral."

Now was as good a time as any to let Whiskey know that Joe Soto was nobody's cluck, either. He said, "As a kid, I was a groom at a Florida dog track. Every now and again, an owner came by twenty minutes before post and gave his dog a little handful of chow. Only it ain't regular chow; it's the kind that expands like a sponge when it hits the dog's stomach. Even a rube knows that's like feeding the mutt a pound of marbles. Damn dog was lucky if he could *walk* all the way around the track. He sure couldn't run any faster than me." Joe Soto slapped his stumpy legs. "And the odds never changed because no one was the wiser."

"Exactly," Whiskey said. "Take a single ball out of a bingo game and the odds go all caty-wampus. Take two out of one column in a blackout, it'd be St. Viator's own miracle before a stiff filled that line." Whiskey jerked the oxygen tube from his face. "Unless you got an ace or two in the hole."

Joe was always smart enough to ask a good question. "Like what?"

Whiskey didn't answer. He lit a Camel.

Joe asked, "Hey, do you go out for breakfast?" He dug a finger into his ear and examined the orange crust, trying to look casual. "Right now I got to go and see a guy, but maybe we should talk some more."

"I eat breakfast every freaking day at the freaking Waldorf-Astoria. What do you think?"

"How about we meet tomorrow at the Tastee-Snack. Breakfast is on me. Say ten?"

Whiskey asked, "What about, for Christ sake? Why the hell are you here?"

"Maybe a business proposition."

Joe needed some time to think it through. Whiskey was sore as hell. That was good. The old guy knew the system—probably knew more than he let on. That could be bad. But the important thing was, he was pissed. If Whiskey didn't get cut in, he could dope out the scam and blow the whistle. Joe knew that meant that someone could be after him forever. But if Joe gave Whiskey a piece of the deal, his odds got a boost. Whiskey wasn't going away. He said he'd be back for the big game.

When breakfast had been served, Whiskey held his cigarette over the ashtray, pinched off its glowing end, and slid the butt into his cardigan pocket. His fingernails were coated with clear polish like a Mafioso chief. It didn't matter to Joe. The scam was solid—better with a guy like Whiskey involved. He couldn't miss for sure.

"OK," Whiskey said, "so what's the deal?"

Joe spelled out the details of the play and then refilled Whiskey's coffee cup from the chipped plastic pot, his hand shaking.

Whiskey said, "You got absolutely the right idea. Count me in. But you got to cut Corner in."

"Why?" Joe didn't like Whiskey juking his plan. The old guy had to learn who was boss in the operation.

"Why?" Whiskey repeated. "Because he handles the hopper. Listen, this is God's honest straight dope. Before a big game, everyone runs for the crapper. They don't wait around to see the balls go back in the hopper from the game before. They sure don't see the couple that a caller might palm. Then the caller signals his guy to grab the cards without those numbers. Get it? Like I said yesterday, them missing numbers make all the difference in the world. Even better when you add a few extra balls with your numbers. It all happens so fast, you never see it, never know where they come from or where the go. Just like you never see that little handful of food expanding in the dog's stomach."

Joe drummed his fingers on the plastic tabletop. The picture was clearing. "If Corner pockets three B numbers, a bunch of cards have no chance of winning."

"Twenty percent," Whiskey said.

Joe slapped his forehead. It was too easy!

Whiskey nodded. "They're out of the picture from the get go. Add those suckers to another fifteen percent of the players who can't concentrate for as long as a blackout takes—you know, it's the end of the night and guys are tired, some of them have been hitting their jug of holy water stashed under the table. You got to understand that bingo is nothing more than the Catholic version of the mob's old numbers game. If you're going to go at it legit, you got a better chance of making money by staying home. But now, with your bunch of guys, you pass the word about the numbers Corner gives you. Your guys root through the card box for the right ones. I'd bet on your organization in a flash."

It was tough to argue with Whiskey's logic. Joe wasn't going to like what was coming, but he had to ask. "What's Corner's take?"

"Twenty percent."

"I'll go ten. I'm only taking half myself. Splitting the rest between the guys."

"No matter how many guys you line up, you *may* get half. With Corner boosting a couple of numbers and maybe adding a couple, you get as close to a guaranteed score as you'll ever get. Your half only drops by a few G's."

"I don't know. Twenty percent off the top?"

"Look, kid, take what you can get when and where you can get it and move on to the next dance. A deal like this comes around almost never. When was the last time you clipped someone for twenty large?"

Whiskey was right as Ringo. Joe Soto had never been close to a scam like this. It was no time to be stupid and pass on a shooter with hot dice. He shook hands with Whiskey, wondering what kind of guy—no matter how old—polished his fingernails.

On the night of the game, Joe confirmed his midnight flight to Tampa. He took a cab to Caribou Pete's Saloon and knocked on the back-room window. The nineteen guys he had lined up were all there. Every guy would handle twenty cards in the big game. They'd meet back at Pete's to split the loot.

At the intermission, three of the guys clustered around Whiskey like apostles. Across the room, Joe could barely sit still. When Corner began calling the fifteenth game, Joe ran to the bathroom and puked.

The nineteenth game was won on six numbers—two N's, a B, an I, a G and one O. Corner slipped Joe a holy card that said N-37 and N-41. It went into his pocket. Joe glanced at the wall clock: 9:50 p.m. Plenty of time. He spread the word to his guys and beat it to the card box, carefully choosing twenty cards without N-37 or N-41.

At his seat, he arranged and rearranged the cards. He saw himself bedding down in some whorehouse near the Tampa Airport after springing for champagne. He'd be sure to tip the hooker a double-sawbuck.

When he thought his stomach would erupt again, he paced the rows of tables, reminding his guys of the victory party at Caribou Pete's. He checked on Whiskey. Corner had just given him a holy card. Nothing got by Joe Soto.

Corner announced the last game with "a prize of ten thousand dollars for some fortunate winner. If they do it in forty-five numbers or less, make it forty-five thousand dollars in crisp hundred-dollar bills to the luckiest lad or lassie since Knute Rockne." The crowd whistled, slapped the tables and stamped their feet, bulls ready to charge the communion rail.

Corner yelled, "First number…under O…O-72."

At 10 p.m., Corner said, "The twenty-third number is…B-7." Lighters flicked everywhere; shaky hands reached for pretzels and boxes of Good 'n Plenty. Joe looked up to see Whiskey staring at him. The old guy adjusted his oxygen tube, winked and lit a cigarette.

Joe got back to business. He noticed that only three N's had been called. By the fortieth number, only five N's had been called. Corner was dead on.

Joe's best card still had six blanks. He wouldn't be winning. He swept the room, trying to catch the eye of his players, trying to see if anyone was close. Everyone was following orders, keeping their eyes on their cards.

"The forty-third number is…" Corner paused and scanned the gray haze that filled the hall. Joe had seen him work the crowd before by slowing down the call as he got closer to the payoff.

At 10:07, Corner took a deep breath. "The forty-fourth number is N-32." The crowd gasped but no one yelled. Joe wondered how many players were one number away from the big payoff. He was three numbers away on his best card. Corner reach for a ball.

Almost whispering, Corner said, "For forty-five thousand dollars, the forty-fifth number is…." He paused to pan the crowd.

"Let's go!"

"C'mon!"

"Son of a bitch!"

"The forty-fifth number is…B-11."

"Bingo, by damn!" Whiskey's left hand shot into the air.

Whiskey waited until the hall cleared before heading up to the stage for his payoff. Joe and the team hustled over to Caribou Pete's and pushed the tables into the shape of a horseshoe.

Corner arrived by cab with Whiskey's five trophies. "A reporter nabbed the old man," he said. "He'll be right along."

Corner aligned the trophies in the center of the horseshoe. Joe broke out the champagne. The guys toasted Joe, their good luck, Corner and Whiskey. The first case of champagne was gone in a half-hour. By the end of the third case, Corner was standing sentry at the window, watching for Whiskey's cab. Joe checked his Timex. He'd have to take a morning flight if Whiskey didn't show soon.

At Anchorage International Airport, Whiskey paid for a first-class ticket with hundred-dollar bills. Once to his seat, he thanked the stewardess who'd helped with his oxygen tank. She glanced at his ticket and said, "Chicago? You've got a long trip."

"I do," he said, "and I'm going to enjoy every minute. Thanks for your help."

"You're quite welcome..." She looked again at the ticket. "Mr. Goldberg."

"Rube. Call me Rube. All my friends do."

He excused himself and towed his canister into the first-class bathroom. He lifted the toilet lid, unscrewed the top of the oxygen tank, and poured in a dozen bingo balls. They bounced around the aluminum bowl before settling down like a cluster of plastic onions. Whiskey spotted two N's before flushing.

The Strength of His Ancestors

Old Amos leaned against the weathered totem pole, his forearm resting on the *Yax-te*, the bear symbol for the Auk tribe. He hardly realized that the charred totem was grinding warm ashes into his forearm. It was dusk, and his hearing and eyesight always faded as day turned into night.

He rested his head on his arm. Scraggly, shoulder-length hair, once jet black but now the gray of ninety winters, hung in untamed tangles. Even breathing was difficult. His lungs cringed at the noxious odor of the wild skunk cabbage that grew in southeast Alaska.

The yellow-flowered broadleaf had been used by generations of his ancestors. Once, his grandmother had plastered his chest with its leaves to treat a violent cough. Later, she had boiled its fibrous roots and wrapped them around a bloodied knee. Its mash was smeared on sprains to take down swelling.

All so long ago, Amos thought. Back when he'd been a proud hunter who wouldn't return to the village without game—a fearless fisherman who could maneuver a log boat within a foot of dangerous rocks, set a net and escape before a wave drove the boat to certain destruction.

Now, it was all gone: the village, the community houses, the tribe. Soon...him. The *Yax-te* totem was all that was left.

He eased himself down the totem's trunk, heedless of the coarse bits of char grinding into his red and black-checkered wool shirt. He sat with his legs in front of him, his bent back against the base of the pole. He inhaled deeply; the skunk cabbage stung the inside of his nose, a smell far worse than the fresh black bear dung he had stepped in ten minutes earlier.

Around him, berries grew everywhere on the floor of the rain forest. Pink salmon berries, bright red highbush cranberries, and blueberries. All growing through a dense layer of silage, the fodder probably as old as he was. Fiddleheads, mushrooms, and wild celery. He'd certainly never go hungry. And if he had to, he could make a bed from the branches of a Sitka spruce or the long-needled jackpine. He could still eat with the hungriest and hibernate with the bears.

He craned his neck to the top of the totem. From *Yax-te* to *Yey-ku-du-hits*, the black-eyed bird. Then the bluebird he had known as *Kla-sque*. *Shushk*—the legendary robin whose breast had turned red when it had hopped too close to the fire in the food pit. The frog monster, the dog salmon, the summer weasel. Proudly atop the pole, the raven, representing his clan from the Dipper House, all once rich and vital. Filled with legends of strength and power. Legends he had been too brash and worldly in his youth to believe. Now, the totem was barely more than a rotted telephone pole, marking a way of life that had long passed on.

Amos dragged himself up from the sacred ground. He had never understood what drew him to the spot. Nothing was here any more, nothing but rain forest between the totem and his cabin ten miles toward town. Maybe it was the childhood memories. They'd become so vivid. He could recall clearly standing beside the totem a half-century before, watching his grandmother hoe the neat rows of her vegetable garden. Not ten paces from where he stood, he remembered, he had received lessons about hunting, fishing, and trapping from his grandfather while they sat on a log carving figures and watching grandmother work the garden.

Dusk had turned into night. He limped toward the road and his old Edsel. One day, he knew, the Edsel wouldn't crank and there would be no parts to fix it.

Inside, he pulled on the headlamp knob. The one working light shined on an animal in the road. Maybe the shadows were playing tricks on him. The animal looked like an eagle; its white tail feathers spanned the center line of the road. No, not an eagle. He shifted the car into gear and inched toward the form.

A boy. Maybe eight years old. Smooth skin drawn tightly over puffed, bronze cheeks. At first the boy appeared to be as dead as the totem. But when Amos approached, the boy's chest heaved. He put his ear to the boy's heart and felt a strong beat. Then he noticed the badly burned hand and forearm, already oozing poison through cracks in caked-black flesh. The boy's unburned shoulder showed signs of muscle. He would be a strong one.

Amos looked up and down the road. Nothing but blackness. He sat on the pavement and gathered the boy into his arms.

What should he do now? How could he help the boy? How did the boy get in the middle of the road? Where did he come from? There wasn't a cabin for miles. His own was the closest.

Amos opened one of the boy's eyes and saw only the white of a halibut. The child was strong but so was the poison. Amos sat and rocked him, looking toward the silhouette of the totem as if it could help.

Amos kicked open the door. He laid the boy on his cot and tugged the chain on the lone, bare bulb dangling in the center of his one-room log cabin. Covering the boy with a bear skin, Amos wondered about his name.

The cabin held a refrigerator, sink, cot, and a Formica-topped kitchen table with one chair. A recliner patched with duct tape sat in the middle of the room under the light bulb. A pair of snowshoes, three fishing rods, an assortment of rusted game traps, and a hundred tools dressed the walls. The only sound was the quiet hum of the generator outside the cabin.

Amos took two sticks of butter from the refrigerator and began to knead them on the kitchen table. For a moment he marveled at how nimble his usually-stiff fingers seemed. They worked the butter until it was as soft as toothpaste.

At the cot, he gently cleaned the burn and then smothered it in butter. If he only had some hooligan oil.

He dampened a towel and soothed the boy's fiery forehead, stroking it until the towel had taken on the same heat as the boy. He continued to rub, tenderly, as if he were stroking a kitten. He smiled to himself when he saw the boy's clean, young, bright-brown facial skin and his own gnarly, shriveled fingers.

Amos was so tired that he wanted to let himself fall asleep, drifting back to the time when he was no older than the boy in front of him, but he knew a single moment of dreaming could cost the boy his life.

He pressed his ear to the boy's chest, this time barely feeling a heartbeat.

"*Yax-te*," the boy muttered.

The boy was losing the battle to keep his spirit. Butter and a cold cloth weren't powerful enough. He had to get him to the hospital.

At Bartlett Hospital, a white-jacketed orderly took one look at the boy, snatched him from Amos's arms, and laid him on a gurney. "Talk to the folks in Admitting," the orderly said, and jerked his thumb toward a row of desks behind a counter.

A woman in a blue pin-stripe business suit peered at Amos over the top of her reading glasses. She sealed her lips in a scowl before asking, "Are you the boy's grandfather?"

"No."

"What's his name?"

"I don't know."

"You don't *know*?"

"No." Amos looked over his shoulder at the boy. Hospital staff swam by, not noticing him. The boy moaned.

"What is your name, sir?"

"Amos Wallace," he said. "Is someone going to help him?"

"Of course someone is going to help him, but we need this information first. Surely you can understand *that*?" The woman removed her glasses, positioned them in the center of her desk, and folded her hands. Her nails were painted bright red. "Can't you?"

Amos shuffled over to the boy. He put his hand on the boy's forehead and felt the fire. He put his ear to the boy's chest, this time hearing a waterfall. "Please?" he said. "I found him on the road."

The woman started to speak. But when her eyes touched Amos's, she stopped and sucked on her lower lip. Slowly, she put on her glasses. She rose, rounded her desk and said, "Yes. Of course," and whisked the boy through a set of swinging doors.

Amos took a seat and stared out the window. Soon it would be winter. He should put the visqueen on the windows right away. And take the chainsaw to some deadfall for next year. He'd had to burn alder last winter, and it had almost roasted him. Find some good hemlock. Yes, he decided, he would do it soon. And he fell asleep visualizing himself trimming out fallen hemlock, the boy sitting on a log, watching him work.

The stern woman in the glasses broke his dream. She shook his shoulder and he came slowly awake. She said, "Sir, the boy you brought in? We're doing everything we can—but I'm afraid his poor little system has just undergone too much of a shock. He's fallen into a coma."

"He's a strong one," Amos said.

As if she hadn't heard him, the woman said, "He has first degree burns all over his right hand and forearm. They're already infected. A nurse is still with him. You can go up if you like."

"Yes," Amos said and followed her through the swinging doors, up an elevator, and to the boy's room. When he saw the boy, he had to grab the sink to keep his knees from giving way. Both of the boy's arms were tied to the rails of the hospital bed. His burned arm lay on a square mat, swaddled in a yellow oil cloth. His left wrist wore a white bracelet. A tube that ran to a glass bottle was taped to his good arm. Another tube led from his nose into the wall. His forehead dripped in sweat, his head swayed from side to side. To Amos, the boy's brown face seemed as gray as ashes. The unknown poison had the strength of a killer whale.

The nurse whispered, "You can only stay a few minutes."

Amos glared at her.

She stepped back and said, "Well…maybe a bit longer. But don't you dare wake him."

As she left, the hall lights dimmed. A wall clock told Amos that it was midnight.

He pulled a wheelchair across the tile floor. For minutes, he just watched the suffering boy. Then he pressed his hand to the boy's forehead. He pried open one of his eyes; it was still the color of fish.

Amos ran his fingers through the boy's matted hair and again saw himself as a youth. Picking the nagoon berries. Catching the salmon. Watching grandmother.

When he awoke, it was three o'clock. The boy's mouth hung open. His parched lips had split, and a trickle of blood rusted his chin. The waterfall inside the boy's chest had turned into a roaring rapids. Amos barely heard a heartbeat. If the poison wasn't released, the boy would die by morning.

Amos paced the quiet hospital room. He could not fight the hag with the glasses. His own feeble attempts at medicine had proven useless. The hospital cure was not helping. Nothing was working.

He leaned over the boy. "I would give you my useless old life if I could."

"*Yax-te*," the boy murmured.

"*Yax-te. Yax-te*," Amos repeated. "What are you saying, boy?"

In moments, he figured out the answer. He walked to the sink, washed his hands, and returned to the bed. He unfastened the ties that bound the boy to the bed and lowered its side rails. Gently, he removed the oxygen tube. Then he peeled off the tape that held in place the feeding tube.

He lifted the boy into the wheelchair and covered him with blankets. After he checked the hallway, he rolled the wheelchair to the elevator. On the ground floor, he slipped out through the emergency door and pushed the wheelchair to the Edsel.

He drove to his cabin for the bear skin blanket. Then he drove to the totem. He placed the boy's limp body against a jackpine and began to dig through the ashes at the base of the totem. No doubt the boy had been playing with matches. The totem had caught fire and the boy had been burned trying to put it out.

Amos continued to dig until he had a hole big enough for a forty-pound king salmon. With a flashlight lighting his way, he gathered a dozen skunk cabbages and lined the hole with their leaves. He placed twenty-one rocks in a circle around the totem.

He laid the bear skin next to the hole and then laid the boy on the bear skin, within the circle of rocks. He lowered the burned arm into the hole and positioned the hand so that the boy's tiny fingers were touching the totem. He covered the arm with more skunk cabbage leaves. Then, for himself, he laid out a mat of jackpine boughs by the boy's head. Finally, he sat down and placed one of his hands on the totem and the other on the boy's fiery forehead.

Amos recalled legends of the Auk tribe. His grandfather had told him of the fierce strength with which his ancestors believed, lessons wasted on a doubting youth. Now, he could no longer afford to doubt. To keep himself alert, he hummed from the old chants that he'd learned from the elders. He hummed the dances. He hummed modern songs from the radio. As he hummed, he rocked back and forth, never releasing the boy or the totem.

As the sun started to rise, Amos continued rocking and humming. Behind him, a rustle in the rain forest broke his trance. He turned to see a black bear standing just outside the circle of rocks. The bear tossed its head and pawed at the damp underbrush. Amos yelled "Yah!" and the bear ambled off toward the road.

Still watching the bear, Amos felt a chill in his hands. Then he realized that the boy's head was cool, too. The color in his face had returned to the bronze of autumn leaves.

The boy's eyes opened. "*Yax-te*?"

Amos glimpsed the bear's flanks as they disappeared across the road. "*Yax-te*," he replied. "*Yax-te*."

The Jade Staircase

From my throne in the grand ballroom of the Sheraton Alaska Hotel, I watch 1,800 revelers gyrating to the music of Stuck Metal Zipper. Of all things, I'm thinking about the post office, about mail delivery. My mail comes addressed to Nino Villaneuva. Only through a sender's sloppy oversight does it come to Mr. and Mrs. Nino Villaneuva or to The Nino Villaneuva Family. I have no wife, no kids. I'm not in love nor do I have a significant other. There's Mother, of course. She has her string of gentleman callers but lives alone and sleeps only with her collection of cell phones. Getting mail—no one ought to be thinking about mail at a time like this.

I'd donated a week of my vacation to oversee the work of the Decorating Committee. Trust me when I say that I was in and out of this ballroom a hundred times a day for seven straight days. I discovered every service entrance, stairway, and elevator in the hotel. In my fifteen years as a display manager for Montgomery Ward, I'd never seen a project so complicated. I've decorated stores from Los Angeles to Fairbanks. I've done seasonal themes for entire malls. On the side, I've designed sets for six repertory companies and eleven high school plays, from *Hamlet* to *Streetcar*. My professional life is adornment; I'm an artist. Yet nothing I've ever done compares to this.

Planning began last year. I couldn't hide the ballroom's massive stage, so I decided to utilize it. I sketched out a wooden ramp, one that ran across the stage from wing to wing. We started building it last Monday. By Friday morning, a forty-two foot Chris Craft was anchored to the floor of the orchestra pit. Imagine the chore I had navigating *that* into the hotel!

I mounted a pair of Louis XIV highback chairs on the boat's bow and voilá—the thrones for the review stand were complete. Over the past twenty-four hours, the Decorating Committee must have inflated ten thousand balloons and pinned up a mile of gold and silver bunting.

When I made my official appearance six hours ago, I was, of course, grandly royal. Anything short of the most regal entrance would have been unacceptable. The yacht rose from the orchestra pit. I was the fabled Phoenix. Now, it's eleven o'clock Saturday night, and I've entered the last hour of my glorious 365-day reign.

My official appellation is: Jason, the Jewel of Jupiter, Emperor XX, His Exalted Dominance of the Alaska High Court. I am presiding over festivities appropriately named *Splendor 2000: Majestic Wonderment Coronation and Charity Extravaganza*. Common name: the gay ball.

My efforts with the decorations have been matched by the guests' work on their costumes. The finery runs a gamut from eel skin to Spanish lace, wax paper to burlap. Some gowns were imported from Europe. One had even been worn by Marie Antoinette, although the wearer confided to me that Marie had far larger breasts than he could ever hope to display.

Unfortunately, my own outfit is causing a problem. I'm in a gold lamé body suit flawed with an agonizing snag on the left thigh. If I stand, I'm afraid the snag will run like cheap panty hose. My empress, Willow Swan of the North, a pastry chef by day, is wearing a gown made from shimmering chains of interlaced beer can pop tops. The silvery strands gather just under his breasts and hang to the floor. When he stands—although I'd never say it—he looks like he's draped in a shower curtain. For the sake of modesty, he's also wearing a sequin boa over his nipples and a matching jock strap to cover his nether parts. I need his help. "Swannie, can you clip this thread without unraveling me?"

His look tells me that I might as well have asked him to sew me an entirely new outfit on the spot. Then, from between golden lips, his tongue flicks like an asp. "We have *people* to do those things tonight. Get Clark."

Clark is the waiter. Clark Gable. Made up perfectly as Rhett Butler, right down to the razored black mustache and formal evening attire. His splash of Drakkar Noir, a robust breath of sea air, would have been beyond Scarlett's imagination.

"Swannie...please?" I say.

He flips the end of his boa in my face and turns his back to me.

Swannie was born Phil Tucker, the brilliant and talented son of Buck Tucker, a now-deceased Chicago house painter. Before Buck's death, he distinguished himself by siring a family of seven sons and four daughters. Phil, the oldest, distinguished himself as an all-state diver on the Fenwick High School swimming team. "Flying Phil," the *Tribune* called him. He won a full scholarship to Notre Dame. Buck moved his family to South Bend and resumed painting houses, hoping Phil would show an interest in football. At six-feet six and weighing all of 162 pounds, Phil was not inclined toward men in pads.

Long after Phil had graduated from Notre Dame, Buck realized what he called the house painter's dream-of-a-lifetime: He was chosen to help gild Notre Dame's Golden Dome. He was so proud that he sent his son a mayonnaise jar filled with the historic golden paint. The jar sat on Swannie's dresser until earlier tonight. Buck would roll over in his grave if he knew that his son was using the paint from Our Lady's dome as lip gloss.

I still need help with my dangling thread. "Willow Swan, this is our final hour of glory," I say. "We have a pecker order around here. I'm the emperor and you're the empress. I refuse to conclude my reign with an errant thread. What would people think?" I adjust a blond ringlet under my ivory crown. After six hours of festivities, my hair resembles that of a sheep dog.

Swannie stares at the dance floor. He continues to ignore me, imperial to the end, his lips tight, the corners of his mouth stretching his face into a nasty pout.

The ballroom steams with a crowd of Alaska's most colorful and generous people: bartenders, bouncers, and bookies; cabbies and cooks; hookers, pimps, and madams; inquisitive liberals and risqué socialites. During rehearsal, Swannie had summarized perfectly the impact of the ball: "Tonight, you won't be able to score smack, snatch, or so much as a football card within a hundred miles of Anchorage." Hell, we even have a table filled with uniformed cops. Of course, they're on their best behavior because their juvenile offender ranch is going to be our most heavily-endowed charity.

"Swannie," I say, "the dream night is about to end. All we have to do is distribute the money and crown our successors. Then Toto and Dorothy can go back to Kansas. Please be nice for a change. Fix this thread."

"I told you—get Clark. Get a *boy* for all I care."

"I don't want a boy, you bitch. I'm gay, not queer."

In his typical clipped tone he says, "What you are is a lonely, whining old hag. There is nothing wrong with you that a linebacker can't fix. You think you have problems? Remember my wife and the three little Tuckers? The ones who walked out on me last year? Now they're threatening to move back in. *That's* a problem."

"OK, I give up. I'll settle for a drink. Johnnie Walker Red. A double. On the double."

"The waiter is on his way, your highness," Swannie says. "Or is it, your *heinie*? I never know which word is appropriate when you get snitty on me."

Phil can be frustrating. He's right about companionship, though. I haven't touched a man in ages. I'm thirty-eight, intelligent and in shape. And I'm the emperor, for God's sake. I deserve a companion.

The trumpeters' first fanfare announces that the incoming emperor's entourage has reached the base of the Sheraton's jade staircase. Soon, the second fanfare will start the entourage on its processional up the staircase to the ballroom.

An hour earlier, the High Court and its honored guests from around the country had gathered on the staircase for the formal coronation night photo. Two days before, I'd personally decided on the location and spent more than two hours blocking the shot with the photographer, entirely missing my pedicure. I picked the staircase for its rich, glossy texture. The jade was as smooth as baby's skin while being noble and tasteful. For the photo, Swannie and I stood on the top step. The forty-two members of the High Court cascaded down the circular steps like a tropical cornucopia of feathers, silks, and sequins.

After the photo, Clark brought out a silver serving tray. It held a chalice and a thousand-dollar bottle of Chateau Moutin-Rothschild, 1945, 'Year of the Victory' printed in French on the label. During the coronation toast, I honored Empress Margaret I, the founder of Alaska's gay community. I could not have been more sincere when I said, "Thanks to the original Empress Margaret, we have finally reached the top of the jade staircase. Nothing is beyond our reach." I raised the chalice in salute. "Only when the wine is freed from the bottle can its nectar be fully relished."

A thunderous ovation rocked the hotel. I was delirious at the response—until some vulgarian pinched my left buttock like it was a lemon wedge. I knew I'd be black and blue by morning.

* * *

I finally snap the damn thread myself. Thankfully, the lamé doesn't run and none of my vitals are exposed. Clark Gable arrives with a snifter of Johnnie Red, and I settle down to enjoy my last regal minutes. To my left, Swannie banters with the crowd. To my right, Clark stands at attention, his hairline mustache glistening with perspiration. He is probably straight as a yardstick, but I can't help visualizing my tongue sliding along the ridge of his upper lip.

Swannie, the ever-helpful one, leans across my lap and says to Clark, "Dismissed. You're dismissed. Go." To me, Swannie says, "Sweetness, we have never so much as looked at each other with a twinkle in our eyes. Yet I admire you so. I wish I could fill the emptiness in your heart."

The Swan needs a taste of his own tartness. "You treat me like a dog-pound cur. You humiliate me in public, then call it admiration?"

"Jason…Nino…whoever you are—don't be a kvetch!" He waves his hand over the ballroom. "Almost two thousand adoring fans are out there on the dance floor—in your honor."

"Swan, all I want is one in my bedroom. Is that asking too much?"

"The waiter is a cute little guy. I grant him to you."

"He's likely as hetero as that late, great house painter, Buck Tucker."

"Maybe you're trying too hard," Swannie says. "Listen to the gospel according to Willow Swan: Love is an accident. Love is God's accident. Love is God's greatest accident. You never see it coming. Amen."

In spite of his attitude, Swannie is sweet and he cares. "You're a good friend, Willow Swan. Your heart is black, but your outfit is stunning." At six-foot six, he'd be stunning in brogans and bell-bottoms.

"You have no idea of the hours I fawned over it," Swan says. "How many gowns have you seen out there for a guy as tall as me?" He throws his hand toward the dance floor again. "Look at them! Kissing, caressing, fondling with abandon. Undulating in orgasmic delight. Most of them are lonely, too."

"They're all in pairs, so far as I can see."

He chucks me under the chin. "All part of the costume, laddie. If you're in drag, you have to be dragged by somebody. The grand march will be six miles long, half of it queenly manhood. Surely you'll find six inches."

He takes my hand and nibbles on my forefinger as absently as if he is tasting an hors d'oeuvre. Then he says, "How about that divine ringmaster with the bullwhip? He looks like Fellini's vision of the Marquis de Sade. I know for an absolute fact that he's unattached. A visitor from the Wyoming Court. Rolande-Rolande of the Sagebrush Rebellion. He's a state legislator who's had the nerve to emerge. He'd be perfect."

"Willow Swan..." My mind flashes to the coronation photo on the staircase and my sore ass. "I know all about the Wyoming Court. It's enough to say that he's a disgusting barbarian."

Swannie beats his feet on the Chris Craft, his pop-top gown rattling on the boat's fiberglass deck. "Tell me more or I swear that I will wet my Louis XIV right here in front of God and everybody and ruin your evening. And I won't wash my hands."

"Didn't you once say that your daddy taught you not to pee on your hands?"

"Nino Villaneuva, don't tease. Tell me this minute about the disgusting barbarian. Exactly how disgusting is he? And does he like tall men?"

"He was the one who pinched me during the photo shoot. I wanted to die."

"You've been saying that for years."

The heart of the evening, the distribution of the charity checks, is at hand. Throughout the year, we'd raised over twenty-five thousand dollars, notwithstanding tactics that were a cross between extortion and blackmail.

We'd make a call, explain the concept of a gay coronation, name the charities that would be receiving our largesse, and ask for a donation. If we felt any hesitation—which we did most of the time—we'd quickly and politely offer to drop by the business with a dozen friends. In full party dress, of course. The hapless capitalist, visualizing his store filled with outrageously-frocked gays, quickly relented. And outstanding Alaskan causes were twenty-five thousand to the good. Except for the ten dollars my devoted empress made me withhold as a snotty message to the National Rifle Association.

As emperor and empress, Swannie and I received thousands of dollars in personal gifts from courts around the country. We each selected one item to keep as a commemorative. The remainder will be turned into seed money for next year's ball. I chose a stunning turquoise brooch from the Arizona emperor. Swannie chose an *oosik*, a petrified walrus penis, from the Fairbanks chapter. During rehearsal, he used the eighteen-inch shaft as a wand. In true Swannie style, he'd said, "No wonder you never see a sad walrus. Look at it, eighteen inches—eighteen divine inches. The very thought takes my breath away."

"My God," he says now from behind his fan. "Jason, look down the line. The adorable creature in the wedding gown and mantilla. He'd be marvelous for you!"

"Your eye-liner must be running."

Swannie shields his eyes with his fan, straining toward the bride. "Why would you say that?"

"That perfect little person is a woman."

"Impossible!"

"Trust me, empress, I wouldn't lie. She is a she."

"I give up," Swannie says. "What's this world coming to when we can't tell the boys from the girls."

* * *

During rehearsal this morning, I'd promised the High Court that my presentation speeches would be short. Now I nudge Swannie. The microphone in the boat's pulpit awaits. We have reached the last page of the script.

"Ladies and gentlemen…and those in between…." I pause to receive the expected hoots. "The moment for which we've been waiting has arrived."

Through clenched teeth Swannie says, "This isn't the moment I've been waiting for, but I guess it will have to do."

We present an oversized facsimile check for five thousand dollars to Ramon Belk, a tattoo artist and the spokesman for the Alaska Cancer Foundation. Ramon has just lost his boyfriend to melanoma. We give five thousand dollars to Howard 'Hot Horn' Harris, a seventy-year old saxophone player who lives in a one-room walk-up with seven cats and a gerbil. Howard accepts the money on behalf of the Juneau Burn Center. We give five thousand dollars to the University of Alaska's Adopt-A-Grandparent program.

Our largest donation, ten thousand dollars, goes to the juvenile offender ranch operated by Anchorage vice cops. I've told Armstrong Zamora, a tough, irreverent narc who'd probably busted a hundred people in the room, that the kids wouldn't get a nickel unless he personally bought a table and filled it with eight uniforms. He's come close enough. He delivers seven officers in formal blue, including Commander Cotton. Zamora, of course, wears his street dress: madras golf slacks, a rose-print sport shirt, a fedora with a plastic palm tree in the brim, and Mickey Mouse shades. As Zamora and the commander make their way to the Chris Craft to accept the check, Swannie whispers through his boa, "Zamora just got divorced for the third time. No wonder. Who'd stay married to someone who dresses in a circus laundry?"

For good measure, Swannie snatches the commander's badge. When he gently pins it onto his sequined jock, the 1,800 frisky gambolers climb to their chairs and howl. The chandeliers begin to sway. Swannie has the spotlight. He holds the last check over his head, the ten dollars for the N.R.A., and shouts into the microphone, "If the N.R.A. is good enough for United Way, then it's good enough for us."

The house lights dim and the spotlights laser in on four trumpeters. Naked except for loin cloths, the trumpeters are totally hairless and without makeup, pale as mannequins. The trumpet herald tells one and all that the new emperor's entourage has reached the main entrance to the ballroom.

Clark Gable approaches, an open cell phone in his hand. This is definitely not in the script. He hands me the phone and points toward the ballroom door. My mother: newly redone blue hair, charcoal and pink bowling shirt. With a date. It is Saturday so she is with—Saturday?—it has to be Rudy, the bald undertaker. The phone trills.

"Mother," I say, "what a surprise. Nice of you to call." She waves wildly from the doorway; Rudy's head swivels like a dashboard hula dancer.

"I just had to stop by your party," she says. "Who is that lovely girl beside you? She looks too tall for you. Is she Catholic? She looks Protestant. Don't tell me she's Jewish or one of those street corner Krishnuts."

"Mother, that's Phil. Phil Tucker. He's the dessert chef at Jahn's. Remember, he created that ten-tier cake for your fiftieth?"

"That's him? But she's...he's wearing—"

"Mother."

"Well, I can't help it. Why don't you find yourself a nice Catholic girl?"

We've been through it a hundred times—from high school, when I admitted being gay, through my coming out party years later. She'd been a single mom with a knack for closing real estate deals. She raised me, an only child, and rode me like a carousel horse until I graduated from the University of Southern California. But she could never quite grasp the reality of alternative lifestyles. "Mother, this is the—"

"Hush your mouth!" She is shaking her finger at me from across the ballroom. "Don't use that word in mixed company."

It hasn't taken Swannie long to figure out the call. He stands on his throne and waves like a navy signalman to Mother. Excitedly, she waves back.

I consider killing my mother or my empress. Maybe both. "Mother, I'm fairly busy now. Why don't you and Rudy go on back to your bowling."

"Come by the house tomorrow." She's still talking as I snap the phone shut.

When Swannie sits down, his shoulders shake so hard that he refuses to look at me. Clark Gable reappears and offers the silver tray to receive the phone. Wearing a smile as thin as his mustache, he leans to my ear. "Patience in the face of inopportune timing confirms true royalty." He winks.

The ballroom darkens. For the final time, the trumpets sound, setting off a round of applause. A scarlet litter, borne by eight rippling hunks in zebra-skin cover-ups, appears in the entryway. Two black forms, each wrapped in a cape of white ibis feathers, recline atop the litter. The new emperor's shaven head glistens. The empress wears a necklace of polar bear claws. The couple graciously accepts its ovation.

I am able to catch Clark Gable's eye and hold up two fingers. In moments, a double Johnnie Red arrives. "You've been absolutely perfect tonight," I tell him. "You must be a scotch drinker. What's your real name? We've been calling you Clark all night."

"Michael," he says. "I drink Crown Royal."

In the darkened room, I try to read his eyes, to see if he is enjoying the evening or just pulling a shift. I have to guess that he's been assigned to us only because he's one of the top waiters on the Sheraton's staff and has the stamina to last throughout a seven-hour party. "I'm Nino Villaneuva."

"Pleased to meet you."

"Are you really?" I ask. As soon as I hear my words, dripping with sarcasm as they are, I realize my rudeness.

Michael just nods.

I can't apologize quickly enough. "I'm sorry. I'm so tired, I can't wait to get this makeup off and collapse with a bottle of Johnnie Red. I'm forgetting the good upbringing I had from the blue-haired lady."

Without a word, Michael steps back and disappears down the ramp. I feel abandoned. Humiliated.

The Swan squeezes my hand. "Jason, when our ship hits shore at midnight, I want you to know that I'm here for you if you ever need anything. Just call."

"When we disembark, Willow Swan of the North, my life is over. Celibacy or suicide are my only options."

Swannie ignores me, saying, "You've been divine. I intend to see that all of Alaska knows it was your work—and yours alone—that was responsible for the record-breaking contributions."

Swannie actually has to dab his ring hankie at a tear. He won't ruin his face, even at this hour. Then his fingers reach to my chin and turn my face toward his. He kisses me with open lips. It isn't a kiss of passion; it certainly isn't one of mere cordiality. Something in between.

Then he says, "I wish I could love you."

Masking my shock, I say, "You bitch. I don't love anyone who uses Dutch Boy for lip gloss."

The litter-bearers move up the ramp as the stage lights gradually brighten. When the new emperor and empress reach us, I take Swannie's hand for our last official act.

Automatically it seems, Michael materializes. Under the full stage lights, he is even more handsome than he'd appeared earlier. His skin is as smooth as oiled silk; his eyes are as deep and dark as the jade staircase. Only when Swannie gives my hand a slight tug do I resume my duties and take the chalice from Michael's tray. With deliberate ceremony, I tip the chalice toward the audience and sip. My eyes blur, a combination of the wine's bouquet, Michael's Drakkar Noir, and the emotion of the moment.

I hang on to Swannie's hand as I motion for the new royalty to kneel. As if in blessing, I raise my free hand over them. "On behalf of all members of the Alaska High Court and Majestic Wonderment Coronation XX, I hereby decree that you, Lance the Great and Dawn of the Virginal Sand, shall preside until the conclusion of Majestic Wonderment Coronation XXI, at which time you shall crown your successors, as rightfully determined by the High Court."

I remove my ivory crown and place it on Lance's shiny head. I kiss Lance and the Swan kisses Dawn. Swannie grins and cups Dawn's crotch. The crowd's cheers shake the ballroom; the cabin cruiser rocks like it's on a rough sea. The new emperor and empress assume our thrones.

In my hotel tub, I soak away the evening and shower off the last traces of the year. I pull on a pair of white boxer shorts and pack my makeup. My hair hangs down, soggy and straight. My cheeks burn from astringent and after-shave. I know that the only color in my face is the blue of the sacs under my eyes. I tighten my stomach; thank God for sit-ups. The body is still good, but it won't last forever. I'm glad to be a deposed emperor.

I slip into a pair of faded blue jeans and a yellow cardigan, wanting only to find a bottle of Johnnie Red and drink myself into a stupor. The wrong way to leave a nine-hundred-dollar-per-night presidential suite, but I'm too tired to care. A freight elevator takes me to the lobby; a cab takes me to a liquor store and back before my hair has dried. Then a knock on the door.

Room service? I hadn't ordered anything. Mother? She'd be pounding on the door with her fists. The knock sounds again. This time it carries a touch of impatience…and a hint of Drakkar Noir.

Sister Skagway

I am Sister Damian Aloysius Geoffrey, order of the Servants of Our Lady. I know of no other way to begin the story of my violent act except with my name. In the end, of course, you must judge.

Almighty God has judged me. I have judged myself—sometimes innocent, sometimes not. The good, if often ill-advised, people of Skagway, Alaska Territory, have judged me. I will not mislead you at any turn of the trail: They found me guilty.

I have appealed my sentence to the territorial magistrate up in Dyea and have been told that he planned to telegraph that appeal, directly if necessary, to President McKinley. If the magistrate received a proper answer, he would travel to Skagway and intervene on my behalf. If such intervention does not occur before sun-up tomorrow, I will be led to the gallows to meet my Maker.

My escort on such a fateful trip will be, of course, Mister Lanny Pinchot, a lawless scoundrel of the first order. For days I have listened to Mister Pinchot's footfall on the heavy plank stairs that rise up from Clancy's Saloon to my cell. Nine clumps up, nine back down. Four times daily. His rhythmic steps are as regular as the cadence in a Gregorian Chant.

If this is my last night, I must write what happened before the truth is lost. I will use the margins of what has been tacked up as insulation to my cell: tattered editions of the *Juneau Journal,* dated as long ago as February 1897, as recently as November 1898.

First, the dimensions of my prison: five and one-half paces wide by three paces deep. One tiny window with seven iron bars. Too high for viewing. In the room's plank door, a hatch half the size of the window has been cut. The hatch opens from the outside only. I am regularly taunted and watched by mean-spirited hooligans.

I sit on a wooden crate once used, I believe, to transport lanterns from Seattle to this territory. The walls hold bare shelves from top to bottom—shelves scored with the circular impressions of bottles removed long before my arrival. The storage room has been the favored hoosegow of that band of cutthroats to which Mister Lanny Pinchot belongs. The smells of life—fumes from pipes and cigars and the slops of beer and whiskey—waft up through my floorboards but, understandably, offer no comfort. I pray that the Holy Ghost will show me a way out of my prison.

What do I deserve? Branded a murderess, I am fed twice daily and then, an hour later, led barefoot from the cell for nature's functions, shackled as if I were a threat to knock down my guard and make good an escape. I have assured my jailers that I have no intention of fleeing—although if an opportunity permitted me to liberate myself from these confines, I should surely take it, in daylight or darkness. There is little hope of such; my shredded habit would give me away in a trice, my filthy wimple serving as a beacon.

Already I can hear the evening's dissipation beginning. The swill of demon rum will turn decent men into debauchers. Even though the stampeders have cast aside their wives and children, they seek nothing more than the fulfillment of an honest man's honest dream. After all, God's house is adorned with gold. Their folly, of course, lies in the devil's own brew that stirs their carnal desires. They drink to excess and trade their stake or their poke for a momentary stifling of the concupiscent urge. *Father, forgive them for they know not what they do.* By comparison, Judas was an archangel.

Eighteen months ago, Sister Carolanne Patrice and I had been assigned to bring the Word of the Lord to the Klondike miners in the Yukon Territory. I was chosen for the arduous task because of my upbringing in the Wenatchee country of rugged eastern Washington State. I am a most able woman of stout pioneer stock, being quite comfortable around rifle, rope, and farm animal. Sister Carolanne was chosen, we surmised, because she was the lone daughter in a family of eleven children and accustomed to labor.

Enroute to our mission, we arrived in sinful Skagway, the gateway to the Yukon gold fields. It was a renegade town of four thousand souls run by a band of dishonest grifters, pickpockets, bunco experts, and ruffians. When the Lord wrote the Ten Commandments, he must have been visualizing Skagway. Within a year, make it May of 1898, a hundred ramshackle buildings had sprung up. Ten thousand more men had arrived—as had hundreds more card cheats, unsavory ladies, and outright assassins. All as guilty as Original Sin, but none more guilty than I. And now my story has leaped ahead of itself.

To reach Dawson City in the Yukon, Sister Carolanne and I needed to cross the treacherous Chilkoot Pass, a thirty-two mile section of trail more horrible than the nether regions themselves. We secured transit with a caravan of merchants and set out along the narrow ledge of a trail in a peppery rain. At Finnegan's Point, we felt the ground shudder. The horses nickered. To a person, we looked down to the canyon below. Had we looked heavenward, we would have seen the beginnings of the slide and, perhaps, have all been able to scramble back to safety. It is enough to say that Sister Carolanne, two merchants, and all the horses fell to their deaths. God planted the solid root of a lodgepole pine in my hand. I squeezed the root as tightly as my eyes and hung on as the slide's gravel rained down. When it stopped, my legs were buried. The men dug me out and found that my Achilles tendon had been sliced and my ankle shattered. So severe was my injury that my leg was spliced to my rifle, a fine 30/40 Krag carbine. It had been given to me as a farewell present from my previous parishioners, who understood the rigors of my Yukon assignment so well. I was littered back to Dyea, and thence further back to Skagway for recuperation.

Oh, I have fully recovered in the ensuing eighteen months, but I fear I shall always drag my left leg slightly off-kilter. Lord knows, it's nothing that I cannot endure. I daily offer up this inconvenience for the repose of Sister Carolanne's soul. Mother Superior, when notified of my predicament, ordered me to remain with the people of this burgeoning pioneer town. Unfortunately, Skagway—thanks primarily to Mister Jefferson R. Smith and his loyal band of ragabouts—heeds neither the word of law nor the Word of God. But I have stayed, ever countenancing the orders of my superiors while witnessing the madness brought on by whiskey and isolation. *Yea, though I walk through the valley of darkness, I shall fear no evil…*

The rhythmic clunk of boots thumps up the back stairs. Mister Lanny Pinchot, that squint-eyed scoundrel, will bring my evening meal for which I am fairly well famished. Quite a fine meal, I should add in all fairness, as it is the same food fed to the bawdy house ladies. Daily, I give silent thanks to my captors for feeding me as well as they feed their harlots. I'm also allowed the use of the bawdy house *salle de bain* twice daily.

"Sister. Sister! You awake in there?" Mister Pinchot rattles the wooden door. "Stand back." Then he opens the hatch and leers in. I see his scabby, unshaven face. He has a mouth full of perfectly white teeth, except for a single black hole where an incisor once was.

"Did you expect that I'd escaped your fortress, Mister Pinchot?"

"No, ma'am. Meaner galoots than you have tried." When not speaking, Mister Pinchot has a nasty habit of filling the gap between his teeth with the pink tip of his tongue.

"You brought my dinner, I expect?"

"Yes, ma'am. Now get yourself in the corner."

I hear him lift the crossbeam from the door. He places the meal on the floor and backs up to the wall, almost as if he expects me to leap at him. As hungry as I am, I want more to know if any word has been received from the magistrate in Dyea. But I dare not ask this charlatan. I will make contact with my confidante at the bawdy house later in the evening. All I say is, "I expect you'll be back in an hour to escort me downstairs?"

"Yes, ma'am. Soapy wants you to have all the comforts of home. He was real sharp on what he told me—feed and fertilize her twice a day."

"Mister Pinchot!"

"Sorry, Sister."

"Can you tell me any news of town?"

"Judge Van Horn's been drunk as a hoot since he sentenced you."

"And well he should be."

"He's the law, ma'am. And you never said you was innocent."

"And I never shall. Do you expect me to lie? Mister Two Chew Calderone was violating that young woman. Innocent? I wanted to shout, 'I took a man's life! This is Mortal Sin. I am a murderess!'"

"Look, Sister, that young woman was a dollar-a-dance slut, excuse the French. The whole town knew it. Now you ain't a bad sort and I'm sorry they're going to string you up, but you killed a friend a mine. I ain't too sorry."

The vision of Mister Two Chew Calderone leaps in front of me. Suddenly, I want neither to eat nor to continue the discussion with Mister Pinchot.

Apparently he feels likewise because the hatch slams shut. His boots thud along the planking and down the stairs.

My violent act involving the late Mister Two Chew Calderone began as a result of children. While I was recuperating, it fell to me to provide for the orphans of Skagway. If you can imagine, this city of less than two years old has produced seven orphans. Far be it for me to be able to sustain seven infants without help while maintaining my spiritual practice. Thankfully, the Lord always has a way of providing. Two of the infants' mothers saw fit to abandon their former shame and come live with me and the children. However, God chose me to be the mainstay for them all. The few Christian folk in town came to our aid, but the mantle of provider fell on these endangered shoulders.

Weeks before, I had determined that I needed a season's fare for the children. Last year, I waited until December, and the snows made returning with the meat—a young, succulent moose—nigh impossible. This year, I vowed to go early. I had ventured almost five miles to the Devil's Punchbowl and had seen barely a track. I said a silent prayer and turned back toward town. It took a goodly time for my prayer to reach His ears, but all good things come to he who waits. As I neared town, I spotted a fine Sitka black-tail grubbing the browse on the city side of Lower Dewey Lake. He was not more than seventy-five yards away. If I got him, I could at the very least field-dress him and return in the morning for the meat.

I unslung the Krag and chambered one of its five rounds. Softly, almost in supplication, I gathered my skirts and knelt on one knee. I brought the valley of the rifle's rear sight to the deer's majestic rack and then pushed back my wimple. I snugged the stock to my shoulder and set the forward sight on his shoulder. He lifted his head but did not seem to notice me. I mouthed, *My Mother, My Confidence*, and touched the trigger. The deer's forelegs collapsed. He rose almost as fast as he'd gone down. Quickly, I chambered a second round and fired. This shot broke his neck.

By the time I'd quartered him, night had fallen. It took all my strength to winch the forty-pound quarters up over pine branches. Each quarter hung like a white ghost in the dark Arctic night, but at least my black-tail would not become wolf food.

I loaded the deer's nourishing liver into my rucksack, shouldered the Krag, and headed to town. I had to drag myself along the trail. My game leg pulsed in pain. At the town's edge, more precisely at Captain Moore's Wharf, I heard a woman's scream. I slipped from my rucksack and half-slid, half-stumbled down the embankment only to find Mister Two Chew Calderone, by light of an oil torch, stomping on the arm of Miss Melissa Bonteller, one of the ladies who had eschewed life in the bawdy house.

I ran toward them, my screams drowning out Miss Bonteller's. Mister Calderone, his greatcoat flapping, his britches at his knees but his long johns covering his indecency, turned and cuffed me a blow so solid that I reeled back and did not know that I'd been struck until I was face down on the bank, my lips flecked with river-bank grit. I made it to my knees and called for help.

Mister Calderone backhanded Miss Bonteller across the face and approached me. I cannot repeat his words. It is enough to say his vulgar stream of invective would have garnered him more than a rosary in the confessional. With both fists he pummeled my head until I fell and rolled down to the water's edge. He hobbled after me and put his boot on my neck, crushing my face into the gravel. I remained perfectly still until he seemed satisfied that I would no longer interrupt his horror. I must admit to saying a silent prayer of thanks for Mr. Calderone. He could have bashed my head with a riverbank rock, but he opted to return to Miss Bonteller. He knelt over her causing her a great scream. Any thought of gratitude toward him vanished.

I located the Krag up the bank and crawled to it. When I had it pointed at him, I shouted, "Stop! For the love of God, stop! Please!"

Mister Calderone turned. Much to my amazement, he snorted. Mucus from his nostrils sprayed across his red beard. He pursed his mouth and…spat at me.

"You can spit all you want, Mister Two Chew Calderone, but you let that young woman be."

"You gonna plug me, Sister Skagway?" He stood up and, quite mockingly, put his hands over his head. "Go ahead. Shoot."

"I know how," I said.

He said, "You don't know nothing about nothing."

I ignored the personal degradation. "Let the girl be."

"She's no *girl*, Sister Skagway. I'll guarantee you that much." He started toward me. I clearly heard the gravel crunch under his boots. The light from the oil torch made his beard glow. I admit to being unsure what to do. Because I had been brought up the daughter of a mountain rancher and quite comfortable around firearms, I never endured a moment's fear when facing an elk or a deer. Now, however, I had a man—even this vile devil of a man—in the sights. Do I shoot him down like the deer? I can't! Miss Bonteller writhed behind him, holding her stomach, whimpering.

"Come no farther."

"Oh, I'll come further," he said, not ten paces from me. "I'll come further and I'll take that rifle for my own, and then I'll take you before I finish with the slut. You don't understand that I'm a deputy marshal. Made so by Soapy Smith himself."

"Stop—please." I was begging him but, I admit, I hit the rifle bolt with all my strength, slamming a cartridge into the barrel. *Jesus, Mary and Joseph, have mercy on my soul.* "Miss Bonteller is not a…what you said. Not any more. Please leave us be."

"I won't leave no one be. Fact is, I'll show you something you haven't ever seen before."

"Stop!"

Five paces away he said, "You don't point a gun at anything you ain't going to shoot." At three paces I fired, but didn't hear the explosion. I do believe to this day, however, some two weeks after the act, that I saw the bullet enter his chest and exit from his back tumbling end-over-end. He did not move, did not fall, but stared down at the hole in his shirt and watched the fabric dampen.

When he looked to me, his eyes were at first taunting then astonished, as if he had just received the secret to the virgin birth. "Sister," he said, and fell onto the embankment, his head crashing face first onto a dome-shaped rock buried in gravel. *Oh Lord, have mercy on me, a sinner.*

Because he was one of Mister Jefferson Smith's henchmen, I was tried by Mister Smith's judge. And here I sit—on a wooden crate that brought lanterns to Skagway, and Mister Two Chew Calderone long since given a hero's burial, a flag draped over his spruce casket. And I still see that round from the Krag tumbling out of him. It tumbled and tumbled....

There were alternative courses of action to my dispatching Mister Calderone. If I really had to fire, I could have shot him in the leg. Perhaps I could have held him at gunpoint while Miss Bonteller escaped. Then I could have fled to town. Or I might have fired one round or two as warning to him—and still have a last round in case the warning failed. So many better choices than the one I made.

Now, the methodical footfall on the stairs snaps my preoccupation. My dinner remains on the plank floor. It is quite cold. I will not have time to eat before being led to the bawdy house. Hopefully, Mister Lanny Pinchot will see the kindness in allowing me to eat after my visit.

The door rattles and the hatch opens. "You awake in there?"

I lift my chin slightly, showing him in no uncertain terms that I am in full control of my faculties and that no amount of incarceration will weaken me. "Yes."

"Ready to go?"

"Quite."

I see his tongue fill the gap between his teeth. Then he says, "Off with the boots."

"Really, Mister Pinchot, don't you think—"

"Soapy says you go barefoot when you go out. That's that."

"God have mercy on him. And you." I take to my lantern crate and unfasten my boot laces.

The nine plank steps are rough on my feet. I fear for splinters, hardly noticing the fall chill. Inside the storm entrance to the bawdy house, I am greeted as warmly as if I were a consort. Upon each visit, the ladies in the parlor wave to me; the gentlemen avert their eyes. As well they should. One lady shoos Mister Pinchot to the bar, passing him to another. She returns giggling about the ease of his distraction. The very notion reddens my face.

Mind you, these are the very same ladies who scorned me over the past year and a half. Now they have taken my plight to heart. They are sympathetic and helpful, warm and caring. Whereas once they were my enemies—quite understandably so because I did nothing to endear myself to them—they are now cordial. Each one came to me and expressed her gratitude for what they call my valiant act. They have even taken in the two fallen-away ladies and the seven babies.

It is delightfully devilish of them to mock Mister Jefferson R. Smith in such a manner. After my conviction, he ordered them to evict the turncoats and the children. But the ladies spoke in a single voice, swearing to him that they would forever abandon their trade if he did not allow this bit of Christian charity in his house.

They told me of his fury, hastening to add that it may have precipitated the unusual rapidity to my scheduled hanging. However, we all laughingly agreed it was, somehow, a raw brand of northern justice that he should be so perturbed. I laughed somewhat quieter than the others but, nonetheless, enjoyed the spirit of the humor.

Tonight, Miss Bonteller, my confidante, shows me to a side room with a wash basin. Outside, another lady stands guard to insure privacy. I embrace Miss Bonteller. She inquires about my well-being—she who had been so brutally beaten by Mister Two Chew Calderone. It was she who took my appeal to the magistrate in Dyea. When I inquire as to a response, she looks at my bare feet, knowing that I am to meet the gallows at morning sun-up unless reprieved. We both understand the meaning of her glance.

A cloud grows in my stomach. Tears fill her eyes, one still puffy from the thrashing. I say, "They'll be no weeping on my account, young lady."

"Are you afraid, Sister?"

"Of death? Not at all. It's the natural way of things. What I fear is eternal damnation for a Mortal Sin. I would be much relieved if I knew without doubt that I had sinned grievously. Surely, I shot an unarmed man. Is that fact enough to condemn me in the eyes of the Lord? I have a free will; I could have taken another path. For certain, I am damned with doubt. I know now I could have done otherwise. At the time, I did not. Alas! I suppose I am doomed to vacillate about my guilt until the trap door springs open beneath my feet."

She clutches me as if I were the returned prodigal. Then I say, "The Lord is just; the Lord is merciful. Pray for the latter so we may meet again in this life."

A rap sounds on the door. Mister Pinchot says, "Time's up, Sister."

I can hardly believe it. I whisper to Miss Bonteller, "You'll be sure to get word to me if you hear anything from the magistrate?"

She says, "He said he'd come to you personally if there was a satisfactory answer to his telegram."

Poor Miss Bonteller looks almost sadder than she did that night on the riverbank. I take her chin in my hand. "Be strong, child. The Lord will provide."

Then I touch her cheek with my lips, adjust my wimple and stride to the door to meet Mister Pinchot. Back in my cell, I eat my cold dinner and begin the Sorrowful Mysteries of the rosary.

When I hear a boot thud onto the first step, I notice the sun beginning to brighten the sky.

Gabriel's Gift

No identical twins were more dissimilar than Gabriel and me. He tricked our mother at birth by arriving a month early. His lungs bellowed at full opera volume, but his little heart sputtered so badly that he spent his first ten days in an oxygen tent. I came neatly and efficiently, no trouble at all to Mother, and slept the first sixteen hours of life. Fifty-three years, seven months, eight days ago.

Our grammar school was a pair of attached doublewide trailers on the outskirts of Kenai, Alaska. I received straight A's from the nuns through eight grades, perfect attendance medals third through the eighth. Gabriel never did better than a B in English and arithmetic. I was an altar boy and won the eighth-grade spelling bee. Gabe played basketball and baseball. The school team took regular beatings from the Peninsula's public schools and from the Anchorage teams, but Gabe always came home, swept my homework to the floor, and told me every detail of the great fun he'd had—regardless of the game's outcome.

Gabe had problems with comportment, too. He liked to fight. Francis Juliani, the undertaker's son who was Gabriel's best friend, once pounded snowballs into my eye sockets. The following morning, Gabriel caught Francis J in the school lavatory and squeezed his head between a toilet seat and its commode. Francis J promised never again to lay a hand on me, and then he and Gabe shared a Pall Mall.

In what became known as the Great Halloween Hoax, Gabe and Francis J quietly slid a gurney bearing a rusted-out casket into the storm entrance of the Holy Transfiguration Russian Orthodox Church during the Hallow's Eve benediction. Inside the casket, they'd placed a homemade dummy, a form rich in anatomical detail thanks to Francis J's early training at his father's mortuary. When the benediction concluded, the first of the departing faithful shrieked and caused a minor stampede from the church. Three valuable icons were knocked from the walls.

By the time Gabe and I graduated from grammar school, he outweighed me by twenty-five pounds. He'd grown tall and broad whereas I'd remained short and lean. But I received the Altar Society's *Jesu Christe* Medal and a science scholarship to high school. Gabe managed a basketball scholarship.

During our high school years, we'd talk disturbingly late into the night, him on the top bunk in his crimson Louisville Cardinals' basketball shorts, and me in my flannel jams burrowed into my sleeping bag. He'd ramble on about growing up and having a big family, being a fisherman, trooper, professional basketball player, or pilot. I told him I would have all those careers and more; I was going into library science.

Gabriel surprised everyone by entering the Russian Orthodox seminary. He wanted a family but also felt a calling to God. Russian Orthodoxy allowed both. And, he claimed, the Orthodox priests seemed to have an obligation to drink vodka. I was good to my word and entered Library Studies at the University of Alaska in Fairbanks.

As a seminarian, Gabe shocked us by dating Mary-Kathleen McDermott. He patiently explained, once again, that dating was perfectly kosher—that was the exact word he used—and fully in accordance with the dicta of Russian Orthodoxy. Within a year of his first date with Mary-Kathleen, they married.

I graduated, a degree in library science tucked smartly under my arm, and went to work for the Kenai Public Library. Gabe took me shopping for my first car. He'd just been consecrated a deacon, so we began the evening with a celebratory dinner—Dutch, of course—but it was my treat for the tip. Gabe tried to talk me into a red Mustang convertible. "Live a little, Michael. You'll fret yourself into an early grave." I explained that I lived a lot through my books. If he'd only take time to read some of the new acquisitions.

"You read my share," he said.

Later, without his help, I arranged financing for a Ford Falcon, four-door, gray.

On the day he was ordained, we had spent four hours inside Holy Transfiguration. The incense made me woozy, and I had to be helped from the church. Gabriel abandoned his ordination ceremony and took me to a neighboring parishioner's home. He poured me a cup of coffee and then peeled off his cassock, alb, stole, and chasuble. Under the ordination robes, he wore nothing but the red Louisville basketball shorts and scruffy black Wellington boots.

That night, with his ordination achieved, the word for the evening became *Nostrovia*, and the song of the hour was "If I Were a Rich Man." He drank more than both our shares of vodka. None for me, of course. I had my position at the library to consider. Gabe kept the party alive with spontaneous bursts of the Cossack Kick in his Wellingtons and basketball shorts. My brother, the priest.

I began writing a treatise I hoped to publish in the *National Library Journal:* "The Eternal Aspects of the Dewey Decimal System." Gabe built a family. By the time my tome was complete—187 pages—Gabriel and Mary-Kathleen had produced three children and adopted five others. At holiday gatherings, it seemed Gabe always had two wriggling forms in his stout arms. He'd toss one into the air like a softball and delight in the child's scream of joy. I'd back away, fearful that he'd drop the child. He never did.

Occasionally, some ignoramus would ask which were his real children. Gabe would wink and pretend to pull a nickel out of the closest child's ear. Then he'd say, "They're all real."

I felt an obligation to tell him that he could expect more rude questions because of the way he was handling his priestly affairs. He'd been celebrating the Divine Liturgy in stores, hunting camps, and road houses, calling the unusual practice Pastoral Universality. He claimed that spreading the Word through non-traditional methods exposed more people to Christianity. It wasn't all that important that they believe in Orthodoxy. Just believe. He once celebrated the Liturgy in an Anchorage synagogue!

The editor of the *Journal* finally called to say that she would use my article, but only as a series and only if I cut it by a hundred pages. That wasn't exactly the news I'd been awaiting but, nonetheless, acceptance was cause for a moment's joy. I called Gabriel. He insisted I come right over for a celebration dinner. He also said that he had a surprise.

I steered the Falcon into his driveway. Gabe, now at least sixty pounds heavier than I, snatched open the car door. "Come on, brother. Come on. Come on. Come on." He almost pulled me from the car. "Wait until you see this!"

"Stand right here." He positioned me in front of the center beam of his two-car garage. "Don't move." He ran to the side door. "Watch." I was expecting a trick when one of the electric doors rose, revealing nothing more than the family minivan. Gabe stood with his hand poised over the button to the second door.

"Gabriel, I know this is a trick. Will you please get to the denouement."

He was doing everything but a jig. He touched the second button.

The other door rose, exposing a wooden box big enough for a refrigerator. The box, lying across a pair of saw horses, seemed stouter than most, the planks unusually thick. But all in all, it was still nothing more than a box with two doors.

Gabe caressed the cover. "Get over here and look."

The wood had been recently cut. Its outdoor scent tickled my nose to a sneeze. I touched a drop of sap and rubbed my fingers together. They felt tacky as day-old syrup. I licked a corner of my handkerchief and wiped.

He said, "What do you think?"

"It's a fine box, Gabe." I refolded my handkerchief.

"It's not just a box." He opened first one door then the second, as if the action proved his point. Inside he pointed out six wooden handles tucked into a corner. "Feel the quality," he said. "Genuine Sitka spruce."

"What in heaven's name will you do with it?"

"Michael, it's my casket."

I emitted a squeak, then became faint. My library was filled with writers who conveyed meaning through symbolism. I was certain my brother was telling me, in his own ribald way, that he was dying. "Your casket?" I back-pedaled out of the garage.

"So…?"

"Gabriel, are you trying to tell me—"

"No, no. I plan to drink a few more oceans of vodka before my trip to see the Head Coach. It's just that…now I'm prepared. Look at the craftsmanship!" He rapped its side. In truth, the box resounded like a bass drum.

Nevertheless, my head hadn't cleared. "Please, close the garage door," I said.

He laughed. "A casket is a great thing to have. It's something you can spend a lifetime in."

"Lifetime?" Gabe had confounded me before. This time, however—well, the only word that came to mind was *doozy* Yes, this was a doozy.

"Not a lifetime, an eternity. And until my time comes, I can use it as a toy box for the kids. Doesn't that appeal to the practical side of your life?"

"No."

"How about if I try working on your well-disguised sense of humor? This casket was a gift from an Episcopalian carpenter. He liked my Liturgy and offered to build it free. Francis J said he made the best wooden caskets on the entire Peninsula. The guy actually made me lay down on a four-by-eight sheet of plywood while he outlined my body with a black magic marker."

"Gabe, stop—I won't listen to this!"

My brother did as he often did when I became upset. He threw his arms around me and gave me a rattling shake. I thought my neck might snap. He said, "Saint Michael, I love you like I love no other man in the world, but you have to lighten up. You are going to die of that feared North American disease: seriousness."

Years later, in January, Gabriel suffered a massive coronary on the basketball court and died instantly. Of course, we couldn't bury him because the ground was frozen. Under the circumstances, we did what everyone did: We planned a spring interment and held an immediate wake.

Gabe was laid out in his wooden casket, the top half of the casket opened. His massive torso was dressed in a freshly-pressed black suit jacket, a black dickey and a crisp, white collar. Francis J had done a marvelous job on the face. Gabe could not have looked better: ruddy cheeks, clipped hair, a touch of a twinkling smile. Two rows of poinsettias were positioned in the form of a Russian crucifix on the bottom half of the casket.

After the wake, Francis J put Gabriel on ice, so to speak, sealing the casket and storing it in the mortuary's walk-in freezer. By April, Gabe shared the freezer with an insurance salesman, a state legislator, and a Labrador retriever.

I remember my brother's burial date well. April 13. It was the date on which the *Journal* published the thrice-revised final installment of my treatise.

Mary-Kathleen and I met the pall bearers at the cemetery. The men lined up at the side of the hearse, and the casket was slid onto a waiting gurney. Francis J placed me at its head, and we guided Gabe across the fresh spring grass to the gravesite.

Then, with one hand, Francis J steadied the gurney. With the other hand, like a choir director, he signaled us to lift the casket. When we lifted, the bottom dropped out. Gabe, still frozen white and stiff as an alabaster statue, fell into the grass at my feet. He was still dressed in the clerical collar, dickey and black suit jacket, his lower half in nothing but the scruffy Wellingtons and crimson basketball shorts.

I'm almost ashamed to admit that I smiled.

Henry Bozek's Perfect Lawn

Ethel Bozek stood on the porch of her A-frame, her arms akimbo, her fists lost in the folds of her faded house dress. Her white hair was rolled in pink curlers, one over each ear for her beaux-catchers and two on her forehead for her bangs. On her feet were her husband's corduroy mules. "Henry!" she shouted. "Dinner in five minutes. We're eating in the living room. My show is on."

Henry Bozek scowled one of those scowls that said, "I hear you. Why don't you say the name of the show to see if I'm interested? I never should have allowed that damn television thing into my house. Alaska is becoming a place for sissies."

"Lawrence Welk," she said, as if she had heard his question. Then she was gone.

The next time she came out, Henry knew, her voice would be a notch higher. She'd interrupt his work. Demand that something be done within two shakes of a lamb's tail. Threaten to climb on the train and leave him. It was always something. She wanted statehood for the territory. She wanted a television set. Yak, yak, yak. He hardly heard it any more.

Henry turned back to the lawn mower and squeezed a line of three-in-one oil onto the cutter bar. If he should live so long, he'd give the mower to one of the grandkids just like his pa had given it to him. His pa. Now there was a man. The only homesteader in all of Alaska to have a lawn as long and wide as a coal car. Cut it every week, rain or shine. Oiled the mower every week, too. Without fail.

The 1898 Acme mower had been built only six years after Henry was born. Unlike Henry, however, the mower was as good as new. His pa bragged about paying $3.50 for it back when the family lived outside Fairbanks. "Quality will outlive you," the old man had said.

"Everything will outlive me," Henry now said, patting the leather-cased conductor's watch on his hip. If he could survive growing up in a Fairbanks homesteader's cabin and working thirty-five years on the Alaska Railroad, he could make it a few more years in an Anchorage A-frame. And have a perfect lawn in the meanwhile.

At least twice a week during the summer, Henry left Ethel in front of her television set and climbed into his old Kaiser. Retired or not, he still liked motion under his feet—a tractor, car, train, boat, even a good dog sled. He especially liked the smooth feel of the Kaiser's engine, a purr not broken by nagging or whining. Or threats. He'd drive up and down Anchorage's streets—not busy Fourth Avenue or Muldoon Road but the side streets—looking for good lawns. He could tell in a minute if a lawn had been fertilized. He knew right off if it had been cut by one of those gas-powered mowers. They didn't shave the grass like the Acme; they ripped a blade in half and spit it out with the sticks and stones and splattered dog turds. Left the blade tips brown.

Since his retirement four years back, he'd found a couple of lawns as nice as his—one out by Spenard Lake and another over to Eastchester Flats. He'd driven back to them time and again. This year, though, the Eastchester lawn had been sadly neglected. Crab grass had taken over; edging was nonexistent. Its flagstone-rimmed garden had gone to seed. It didn't take a whiz kid to figure out why.

He pushed the Acme into the storage shed and picked up a rake. Back in the front yard, he measured the height of the hedge against a notch he'd carved into the rake's handle. The hedge kept a few of the visiting moose off his lawn, but now it was a good two inches above the notch. Three or four hours of trimming. Winter was coming. When all the leaves were down, he'd get after it. Once clipped this time of year, it would stay as square as a row of brown concrete blocks until the spring buds sprouted. Maybe he should just go the way of all the newcomers and dig it out. They liked their wide-open spaces. Keeping it trimmed was backbreaking but digging would be worse. Statehooders could go straight to hell.

"Henry Alan!"

He dropped the rake.

"Dinner's on." Ethel's voice pierced the September evening like a honking goose headed south.

He fanned the air with the back of his hand, dismissing her.

"Your old lawn can wait," she said. "Dinner is getting cold, and my show is on."

"Coming," he said.

"If you're not in this house inside of two minutes, I'm leaving you for the milkman."

Henry began raking. If he had a nickel for every time she'd said that she was leaving, he'd be a rich man. She was going to leave him for the milkman, run off with a Chinaman, have a fling with George Burns. What the hell, it was his money bought the food, paid for the A-frame. He had earned it all and could do exactly what he set his mind to doing. Still, he thought, she'd never before threatened to leave if he didn't show *inside of two minutes*.

If she took off, he could check more lawns and not have to face her carping. He could go up to Fairbanks and look at the lawns back home. With the ninety-degree summers up there, Fairbanks had some lawns as smooth as the velvet on a moose rack. Maybe he'd go down to Juneau and Ketchikan to see firsthand what all that rain did to grass. Maybe go all the way to California. He'd never been farther south than Seattle, and made it there only once for Ethel's female surgery. He laughed out loud, thinking about what he'd write on the postcards he'd send her.

The problem was that she just never gave him a moment's peace. She talked backed when he corrected her. She wisecracked like a smart-aleck punk. On the train, Henry could muzzle a jabbering passenger just by hollering about a bear on the track bed. That didn't work with Ethel. She yakked about everything from the weather to the need for streetlights to the trashy element of people moving into the territory. If she left, he could watch the old ball games without going down to Pioneers' Hall. See the fights, too. On *her* television. Hah! He started singing the Gillette theme: "To look sharp…and feel sharp, too…use the razor…that is built for you…"

Henry rested against the rake. His fingers stroked its worn-smooth wooden handle just as they had stroked Ethel in years gone by. On his right hand, a white scar angled between the knuckles of his thumb and forefinger, a permanent reminder of his run-in with the cow moose back in '46. The engineer had been an hour late out of Seward. The train came onto the cow with her calf near Whittier at Tillion's Turn.

The engineer stopped in plenty of time, but it was Henry's job to clear the track. He hadn't seen the second calf and got caught between mama and baby. She charged and tossed him up over her hump like he was no more than a snowball. About ripped the thumb right off his hand. As far as he was concerned, the only good place for a goddamn moose was in a goddamn pot.

Henry toted a bushel basket half-filled with cuttings toward the storage shed. He needed only to sweep up the last of the shavings. He paused, closed his eyes, and saw President Eisenhower lining up a putt at the edge of the lawn. The putt was long, maybe forty feet, but not impossible. The grass was flawless; it would hold a perfect line. He knew this even though he'd never struck a golf ball. Some things a man just knew.

Sweeping was his favorite part of the job. The finishing touch. The perfect end to a perfect lawn. He couldn't understand why everyone didn't sweep their lawn. He always swept across the slant of the grass to erase mower marks.

Ethel appeared on the porch wearing her Sunday coat, the brown wool one, the Easter hat that looked like a bird's nest, and her favorite walking boots. She had her pocketbook hooked through her arm. Their largest suitcase, a nubby-leather Gladstone, was at her side.

"I'm leaving you," she said. "Your dinner is in the ice box. Bottom shelf. In wax paper. My house key is on the top of the bread box."

For thirty years, Henry had been ready for this moment. If she ever started to go, he'd just say, "You ain't going no place." Now, her story about dinner being in the icebox...well, it threw him off. If she'd taken the time to wrap his dinner, maybe she really *was* leaving. He asked, "What did you make?"

"*Pierogi z miesem.*"

Meat dumplings. His second-favorite meal. "Did you eat?" he asked.

"No." She gave her hat a pat and bounced the Gladstone down the wooden stairs. Listing to the right from the weight of the suitcase, she made her way down the packed dirt of Coffee Trail. Henry watched her until she turned onto Division Street and disappeared. He stared at the empty street.

When he finally got around to eating, the cold *pierogi* tasted bitter. It didn't carry the zesty tang of her sauerkraut nor the fresh smack of her homemade horseradish. It was almost sour, like curdled milk.

By God, he'd take himself over to the Arctic Ptarmigan for one of Richard's good kosher hot dogs. He'd do just that and not have to ask anyone or tell anyone where he was going or what he was doing.

At the Ptarmigan he made it through two bites of the dog—no piccalilli, extra onion, and a double shot of celery salt—but it didn't settle. He drank half his cherry Coke before waving at Richard. "Wrap up the rest. I ain't so hungry as I thought. And give me another one to go."

"The same?" Richard asked.

"No," Henry said. "This one with everything but onion. Extra piccalilli." Ethel ate enough piccalilli for a dozen people. Piccalilli on moose, on *kielbasa*, on caribou sausage. Richard wrapped the hot dog in a napkin, snapped open a white sack, and handed it to Henry.

Henry crossed Division Street and took his time walking down Coffee Trail, tipping his cap to Mrs. March, the neighborhood widow who'd grown stooped in the two years since her husband's passing. He wondered if he looked different now...now that *he* was alone. He looked at the log cabin next to Gronkowski's. The haunted house, the kids called it. The old man who owned it was letting it go to the dogs. He could at least pick up the old newspapers that blew onto neighbors' property. Cut the bushes. Trim back those lilacs. Damn lilacs—overgrown weeds is all they were. It was a crime.

Maybe now was the time to visit California. Ethel once saw a show on the television about San Diego. Glorious weather all year, she said. The lawns were *nonpareil*. That was her word: *nonpareil*. Ethel said Henry's lawn was the nicest one in Anchorage, but everyone had nice lawns in San Diego. If he went down there, Henry was sure he'd have a lawn as good as anyone on the West Coast. In time. Things like lawns took work. Patience. Even kindness. Hadn't it taken him years to get his just so?

He was at the edge of his lawn before noticing Ethel on the second step of the porch, sitting on her handkerchief, the Sunday coat folded around her legs, her ankles crossed. The Easter hat sat atop the Gladstone. She said, "I locked my key inside."

"On the bread box," Henry said. He checked the watch on his hip. "You been gone over two hours."

"I walked down to the depot."

"You eat?"

"No."

Henry waved the white sack. "I got a good kosher dog from Richard."

"You didn't like the *pierogi*?"

Henry didn't want to answer. "I went for a walk, too."

Ethel said, "A good dog from Richard, you say?"

"Extra piccalilli," Henry said. "Just like you like."

"Maybe I'll try a little onion next time."

"Onion?" Henry said. "Remind me." He could get her onion. He might not like how it made her breath smell, but he could get it for her. She just had to ask.

About the Author

Bill Miles

Bill Miles has lived and worked as far north as the Arctic Ocean in Alaska and as far south as McMurdo, Antarctica, at jobs ranging from truck driver and bartender to advertising executive and legislator. Along the way he's been a sky-diver, snowmobile racer, boxer, and pilot—all, he says, with remarkably little success.

Bill's fiction has been published in numerous literary journals, and his articles have appeared in the *Anchorage Daily News*, the *Anchorage Times*, the *Chicago Tribune*, and the *Los Angeles Times Book Review*.